4877

Heather Hughes-Calero
THE SEDONA TRILOGY
— Book Two —

Doorways Between the Worlds

Presented with love . . . in SUGMAD.

Coastline Publishing Company
California

1985

THE SEDONA TRILOGY

Book Two *Doorways Between the Worlds*
By Heather Hughes-Calero

COASTLINE PUBLISHING COMPANY
Post Office Box 223062
Carmel, California 93922

Cover design by Lois Stanfield.

Library of Congress Catalog No.: 85-89057
ISBN: 0-932927-01-7

To my mother and father

CHAPTER 1

Sarpent the Chief Elder was on the platform at the Bell Rock gathering place by himself, the other elders departed along with Hanta. He too should have left and been attending to the business of the Silent One.

But he held back.

Something was stopping him, it seemed.

But what?

He moved slowly around the platform, running his fingers over the tracings along the back wall, turning to gaze at the stone bench where the Elders waited during appearances of the Silent One. Then, absently, the Chief Elder went over to the rise in the center of the platform and stood looking mutely at it.

Hanta was soon to translate, to be with them no more. Soon he would never again ascend the steps to take his place as their spiritual leader. But did it matter? Hanta was merely a title given to a state of consciousness, and not the personality of the one who acted as the vehicle for the consciousness. The vehicle—the body of the man in service as Hanta was old and worn out. It had been more than a hundred years since the individual had assumed the Power. No one even remembered his name. He was Hanta, the Silent One and no other identity suited him.

Sarpent looked away, his eyes tracing the steps which led to where Hanta had been. Why then was he troubled?

What was holding him?

Suddenly it struck him. A slow, deathly feeling crept through him.

He was afraid.

Afraid of what?

If Hanta were to translate, who would take his place? It was indeed a great sacrifice as well as an honor for anyone to accept the title. Bearing the name of Hanta was a yielding of all personal life; to be a Godman in the name of God; to relinquish the right to die; and to live as spiritual leader until released at the next Awakening Day or one hundred years hence. And there was more to the task, Sarpent knew. He had served the Hanta long enough to know that the most difficult part was that which could not be told; that which he had only suspected but had never been told.

A slow rising sensation suddenly rushed through the Elder's veins. It was a feeling that had memory within him but the memory was old, from long ago. He tried to listen to its call; to remember its meaning but the more he reached toward it the more intense it became.

What was it?

What did it mean?

Slowly, he heard the answer rise from deep within himself. It was fear. He was afraid. He had known it all along. Suppose he were asked to be the Hanta, would he accept? Could he? Perhaps there would be someone else to take the Ancient One's place. But who? He, Sarpent, was the Chief Elder and highly respected among all the people. Of course, there was Ian, but Ian was not much more than a boy, and one soon to be married. No, Ian would not be suitable for the job. There was no one else that he knew.

Then he remembered.

At a distant village to the East there was a younger man than himself named Casmir. He was said to have benefited the Silent One with great work in the inner realms, and though he was seldom seen in public with the Hanta, he served him well as an emissary for the Askan at work in the inbetween worlds.

Perhaps.

Sarpent tried to imagine himself in service to Casmir. He knew so little of him that an image of the man would not come to mind. Casmir was not an Elder and, like Ian, had no official status in the community. But did that matter? Sarpent was ashamed that he would think such a thing. Hanta was the most humble of beings. His position was one of divine love and not personality. Still, that low rising fear crept forward in Sarpent again. Perhaps he would be chosen to succeed Hanta. He dared not think it. He tried to quiet his mind; to eliminate any thoughts at all on the subject. It was not his place to think on these things, yet Sarpent could not help it.

The sound was persistent, both ancient and alluring. It came in one long wave and did not yield itself. Deetra listened, certain of what she heard, aware that it was the primordial force of all life.

The sound was a deep haunting hum and it was coupled with a distant thin-high pitched sound. It was not the first time she had heard *it*. *It* was with her constantly whenever she wished to be aware of *it*, only now there seemed no way to distract herself from *it*. It was as though the Hanta's physical body was present. The idea struck her. She looked about, knowing full well that Hanta's spirit might be present but that his body was not. There was just she and Ian, who was resting quietly in the next room. She arose, the sound within following in her, and went into the next room to look in on her beloved.

Ian was lying quietly on his back, eyes open and gazing toward the ceiling. He was smiling beautifully as though he was seeing something wonderful.

The haunting sounds continued humming.

[*3*]

"Ian," Deetra called softly.

Ian slowly turned his head to face her but said nothing.

"Do you hear the sound current?" she asked.

His eyes glittered at the question, answering yes, but he did not speak.

"It is the sound of the Great One's presence," she said again.

Ian nodded lovingly.

Deetra studied him. Ian was not acting strangely. She had often seen him retreat to periods of contemplation as she frequently did. She knew he heard the sound current as she did and she saw by the glow in his eyes that he recognized the melody of Hanta. After flashing her a warm look, he turned his head again to gaze sweetly at the ceiling.

Deetra left the room.

Deetra went to a small box she had carefully put away on a high shelf at the far end of the sitting room. Then she sat down on the thick rugs scattered about the floor and opened the box.

In it was a tiny round crystal.

She lifted the crystal from the box and held it up to the light, gazing at and through it, an array of colors dancing about her. It was beautiful, and more beautiful yet were the many experiences it had brought her; how she had learned first to use the crystal and, in learning its power, became the power; how she had put the crystal aside because she no longer required it. The power was hers'. She was the power of the crystal. The sound current flowed richly about and through her. She had become a channel for the Divine Force.

It used to be, Deetra remembered, that she was coddled somewhat. She recalled her adventures on Moonwalk, of trying with Rian and Curtser to save the villagers from the negative powers of the Pink Prince. In those days Hanta and Ian were everpresent to strengthen her. Now, although help would be given if she asked, she was to stand on her own. She recalled how she had progressed to that state and thought of her companions on that journey to the City of Light, to Awakening Day.

There was Rian, the orphan reared by Sarpent, who was given his crystal directly from Hanta's hand. Rian had the ability to recall passages of scripture at the exact moment they were needed for a given situation. It was only fitting that he was now honored in the service of the Elders as Scribe.

Curtser had been less helpful and more troublesome on that journey, although his courage had been commendable. After all, it was he who raised the jewel from the Pink Prince's dagger, and he who had the nerve to draw from it the Prince's secret powers of creation. She had not seen him since Awakening Day, but she heard he had been sent to an Eastern village. Deetra did not know what he was doing there.

It all seemed so long ago, as though it had happened in some ancient time. And it was remarkable to her, looking back, that as frightened as she often was, she was equally inwardly strong and persistent. It pleased her and it had pleased her father Starn. Most of all it was the effort to realize herself an Askan.

Deetra recalled how the name Askan terrified her as a young girl, remembering tales of the Askan power to transmute form, and now she was Askan herself. The comedy of illusion. She was the Askan, yet now she realized that where she was in her spiritual training was only a stepping stone along the way. She and Ian were lovers, soon to be married to become partners on the path through life. Their union, she knew, would be magnificent beyond words, beyond dreams. Their love stretched her in a sense, lifted her, yet although she was nurtured by Ian's love, empowered by it, she sometimes felt dwarfed by it.

She replaced the crystal in the box and returned it to

[5]

the shelf. Then she sat down, tried to relax, to listen to the haunting melody of the spheres.

It seemed that Deetra was taken within the sound, and within there was a strange nothingness. The hum, which was not a music and yet it was, was all there was—that and light. But the light was so intense, so all encompassing that it was past the point of existing. The music came from the greates depth of all life. It came from the void. There was all and there was nothing. Yet the nothingness was intense.

The lack of anything in that void made the intensity unbearable. Consciousness fettered by mind and body could not exist here. Deetra had entered a world beyond herself as mortal. She had somehow slipped beyond herself, beyond everything and everyone—but how?

The answer came from somewhere within. It crept along the edges of her beingness like a warning friend. She had followed the sound of the void and entered into it. It was the Hanta's sound; the place where the Hanta consciousness functioned. It was the powerhouse from which creative energy began.

But why was she there?

Why was she allowed to be there?

The answer came again, but she could not break it into words. It was because of Hanta she was permitted there; because it would be necessary for her to function as a co-worker in some way, and because she had earned being there.

Then, as easily as she had entered the void, she felt herself easing out of it, as though being drawn back into the lower planes. The intensity eased and left her. "Deetra, my love," she heard a voice calling her.

She opened her eyes.

It was Ian, kneeling on the rugs next to her.

"We have company," Ian said softly. "An Eastern tribesman, Casmir, is here to see us." He took her by the hand and helped her to her feet.

Deetra looked steadily into the warm deep-set brown eyes of the Easterner. She knew him or felt that she did. It seemed somewhere, sometime long ago they had met.
But where?
"Perhaps on Moonwalk?" the youthful tribesman said, speaking her thought.
"Perhaps," Deetra said absently. She was thinking of Moonwalk, absolutely sure she had not met him there.
"Your business," Ian said to Casmir, "is urgent?"
"Somewhat," Casmir said seriously.
Deetra could not take her eyes from the young man. It was not his beauty that held her. Ian too was beautiful. All the Askan were beautiful, filled with an inner radiance that shined outward. It was the all too familiar appearance of the man. There was something about him, something she could not quite put her finger upon.
"Well, let's sit down and discuss it," Ian said warmly, motioning him to be seated on the plush rugs at the far end of the room. "Deetra, would you please make us some tea?"
The request startled Deetra back to herself. Her eyes met Ian's and she smiled gratefully, then turned and left the room.
"Tell me of your village," Ian said. "I have not visited there since I was a small boy and I'm sure many things have changed."
"Indeed they have," Casmir said lightly. "For one, the people are multiplying quite rapidly, which means the Elders are busier than ever making sure that the necessities of life are increased and adequate."
Deetra returned with the tea and handed a cup to each man and then sat down next to Ian.
"Is supply a difficulty?" she asked Casmir.
"No," Casmir said, "this is a fruitful time for my vil-

lage. As quickly as the people reproduce there is adequate supply for all."

"Then there is harmony," Ian added.

"Yes, there is harmony for now."

Deetra tried to focus on the conversation and not to permit her thoughts to wander. Whether or not she recognized their visitor from somewhere else or some other time did not relate to the purpose of his visit. He was here to discuss some important matter with Ian and it was her place to be supportive and attentive.

"You will soon be married," Casmir said, turning his attention to Deetra.

Deetra could feel the blood rise to her cheeks, and her reaction embarrassed her even more. It was not his acknowledgment of their planned marriage that overwhelmed her, but a slight mocking quality in the tone of his voice. She must be mistaken, yet she could not answer him.

"When it is time," Ian answered for her.

Casmir nodded knowingly, turning his attention to Ian. "You know the Hanta is soon to translate."

"I have heard the rumor," Ian answered, "but I have also heard the rumors of many things."

"I believe that it is more than rumor," Casmir said again.

"In what way?"

"There has never been a memory of a Hanta to live on long past Awakening Day. After all, the job is done. A hundred years is long enough."

"There is no rule to that," Ian said earnestly. "And I do not believe that it is up to us to establish one now."

"And indeed I agree. I am only doing my job."

"You are here in an official capacity then?" Ian asked.

"I am here because I know that Hanta is to translate," Casmir said. "As a co-worker on the inbetween planes, I am carrying out my responsibilities."

"And we are appreciative of your dedication," Ian said

graciously.

Deetra looked to Ian, somewhat surprised by his sudden change in manner. Did Ian feel Casmir to be his superior? His thoughts were still and so there was nothing additionally to interpret. But then Ian was a master at stilling his thoughts and she knew she would be wise to exercise that control herself. Then she remembered the intensity of the sound current, the hum, as though the Hanta himself had been in their presence at the time of Casmir's arrival. Did it mean that Casmir was to replace him, to become Hanta? Quickly Deetra put a clamp on her thoughts.

"There is something you can do for me," Casmir said. He raised his eyes warmly and gazed at Ian.

"Anything," Ian answered sincerely, "anything at all."

Deetra could not believe she was hearing correctly.

"I will require your support," Casmir said.

"You have it," Ian bowed slightly.

"And may I have yours as well?" Casmir asked, turning lightly to Deetra.

Deetra hesitated, glancing at Ian who offered no suggestion. She knew what was being asked of her. Casmir was implying that he was to be Hanta, or so it seemed. There were no underlying thoughts in his mind to suggest anything more than what he actually said.

"As Hanta wills it, so it shall be," Deetra answered after a time.

Casmir smiled and nodded appreciatively. He rose to his feet. "I must be on my way. The Silent One has much for me to do this day." Then he turned, paused, and turned back again, looking directly at Deetra. "I almost forgot," he said, "I bring you greetings from a friend."

"Who?" Deetra asked, suspiciously.

"Curtser. He is well and sends his best wishes to you."

"Is there nothing more?" It had been some months since Deetra had had news of him.

"Nothing more," Casmir said thoughtfully. "This is

[9]

the only message he gave me for you." Then he looked away, catching her with a light smile, raised a hand in greeting and left.

Ian stood next to Deetra, looking with her at the figure of Casmir hurrying down the road. Her thoughts were still and Ian was pleased that at least his beloved's upset was not grinding away mental images at their departing visitor. Still his presence had disturbed her, her emotions had been hooked. It was only a matter of time before her thoughts raged out of control unless he helped her.

"My love," he said, gently turning her to face him. "Do not wonder about your feelings for Casmir or memories of when you last met him. If you were to push the answer forward at this time it would bear the retribution of impatience. It is not necessary for you to know what you wish to know now. It would only empower his image in you. Move calmly into the next moment and let this one pass."

She drew in a deep breath as though some great burden had been lifted, then smiled. "Thank you. My mind was nearly out of control. It is what I am trying to learn."

He nodded in understanding. "And that is why you were tested," he said.

"It is so very difficult sometimes."

"I know."

"Did it take you so long to master your mind?" she asked.

"It seemed that way." He laughed. "Don't worry about it. It will come. One day you will be surprised. The control will come naturally. Meanwhile, remember your exercises."

She had forgotten. It was so easy to slip and forget the exercises for mind control. All she need do is to place her attention on the spiritual eye, that point just above and between the eyes. It was the seat of the Hanta's presence and as long as her attention was placed there, her mind was under control.

Rian stood looking out the window of his small office at the rear of the Elder's sanctuary behind Bell Rock. The view was pleasing, filled with the vast mountain ranges to the East. Just beneath them was the forest where he, Deetra and Curtser had befriended the wood-creature Dales. How he suffered in those days, desiring love and not knowing how to content himself. Now he belonged. He was given position within the Elder's sanctuary. It was his responsibility to copy the sacred scripture from the notes of ancient Hantas, some of whom had lived eons past. Every successive Hanta added to the scriptures in some way, some more than others. It seemed they brought it up to the clarity of the time, unfolding bits and pieces as humanity readied itself. As yet, there were no markings left by the current Hanta, but Rian knew that the Godman was preparing his scripture now. He also knew that it was customary for Hanta to translate after this last great task was completed.

Rian turned and paced the floor near his writing table, studying the stacks of texts completed by other scribes. Hanta's translation was of grave concern to him and his concern was personal. Rian remembered and the memory again brought tears to his eyes. Long ago, when Hanta had given him a crystal, Rian had wanted to thank him but the Ancient One had given it without looking at the boy, had actually turned his head from him. Rian could not forget. The rejection he felt today had festered inside him since he was a boy. And yet, Hanta himself had given him the crystal. He should have felt honored. It was a rare act for the Mighty One. Even Deetra had received her crystal from an Elder.

Rian returned to his seat at the table and unrolled a scroll he had not previously read. The honor of his privilege to work with the ancient texts was overwhelming to him. He was trusted to copy the hands of many Hantas. How could he feel so bereaved by a simple turn of the head. Glancing at the text, he began to read softly aloud.

*When a person discovers who he truly is,
he becomes more relaxed and more natural. It
is not odd that others are drawn to him or listen
with bent ear to discover his secrets.*

Rian paused in his reading. The next line was written in a different hand:

*Their secrets are that of the vast reaches of
space, the void understood only by those who
have the mark upon them.*

Something in Rian bolted.

Mark?

What mark?

Who had added that phrase and by what right?

Rian scanned the scroll further for a clue. Nothing else was added to it. He picked up another scroll and then another, examining them. Nothing had been added. Then he drew another. His breath caught. The entire scroll was written on the subject of the mark. In the margins were notations in the same handwriting as the previous notations. Someone had tampered with the scroll, adding to it in brackets.

Rian began to read:

*The mark is that initiation which binds one
to the inner master* (or seat of consciousness
within the worthy one). *It is the power, the wisdom, and the love bestowed upon those who have
proven their readiness.*

*The mark is visible to all who approach and
yet its form is formless.*

*The presence of one who wears the mark is
graceful with power, wisdom, and love* (which
is charity), *and all who approach recognize this.*

*Recognition of a mark-wearer does not
mean that he who recognizes will accept* (without
question or rebellion). *The rebellion may be
fierce, such as the attraction of an opposite*

[*12*]

force.

*They who wear the mark are the chosen
ones and are protected by the positive forces* (as
long as opposing thought does not invade). *It is
the responsibility of the mark-wearer to exercise
control* (at all times).

(The mark, once placed, can never be removed.) *It is the heaven of he who serves the
Divine Forces and the hell of he who finds he
cannot.*

Rian reread the last paragraph once again, noting that
the mark was said to be indelible. He then was a wearer of
the mark and he knew from his own experiences the glory
of service and the hell suffered when there was none to
give. He flashed on an image of the Pink Prince, the negative force, which had once held him captive and then
quickly dismissed the image from his mind.

But who had said the mark was indelible. It was written
within the brackets by a different, imposing hand. Who had
added the notations. He read down the page to study the
signature of the original author. It was simply signed Hanta
and the date was some thousand years ago. The author of
the notations had not identified himself.

CHAPTER 2

Deetra hurried to the village gathering place, where once a month she met a small group of villagers to instruct them in the message and meaning of Awakening Day. It was a task she loved and yet the challenge sometimes appeared to be exceedingly great.

Those Deetra instructed were those who were learning as a result of Awakening Day, beginning now to prepare for the next. It seemed to ease their anxiety to know that it was a hundred years forward in time; that perhaps they would go so far in this life and pick up at that point in the next. This freedom encouraged many.

Deetra thought of herself, meeting Ian three moons before the great day. There had been a terrific urgency in her preparation. Perhaps she, like them, had begun in a previous life. Perhaps her story would also be their story.

She paused beneath the eastern cliffs of Bell Rock. Their crimson towering majesty always seemed to excite her. It appeared filled with mystery and, to the uninitiated, it was. The platform had held the physical form of spiritual giants, Hantas throughout the ages, and the memories of such memorial events were collected invisibly there.

Deetra took a seat on a rock just beneath the platform, closed her eyes, and waited for the students to arrive. The sound current, the beautiful music of the spheres, lured her into contemplation to a time when Hanta had last met with her. He was on the platform above with Ian at his side. It was Awakening Day. It was her moment in time suspended.

The moment was a moment of consciousness. As she stood looking up at the radiant form of Hanta she had realized all the balance of life, of herself as limitless Soul, and in an instant she saw how she could tap into that state of beingness while living, aware of her physical form and its inter-relationships with the environment.

She opened her eyes.

Seated about her in a semi-circle were those who had come to learn spiritual law. They sat with eyes closed as if tuned in to her great drama.

Deetra wondered and instantly knew.

"Tell me," she asked of the man Tolar who sat across from her, "what images came to mind while you were waiting for me?"

Tolar looked about at the others, uncertain. "I'd rather not say," the man answered.

Deetra looked at the others. They were looking critically at Tolar, as if he was hiding something from them.

"Was anyone here thinking on the Hanta?" Deetra asked, looking from one to the other. She could feel Tolar's attention heavily upon her.

No one spoke.

"I was," Tolar said finally. "I was remembering a time when I had seen him sitting on his bench at Tower Rock and I wondered why I had not seen him since."

"I believe we are not to question such things," Geta said quickly, hoisting herself up on her knees. "It is dangerous to wonder such things, and it is a sacrilege."

"In what way?" Deetra asked.

"Well," the girl began hesitantly, looking to the others for support, "it's well known that Hanta is not like us, therefore we cannot understand his greatness. It is not right, and it is dangerous for us to try to do so."

"I see," Deetra said, deeply studying the girl, wondering how to reach her. "Tell me Geta, have you ever seen Hanta?"

"I mustn't think of it," the girl answered sharply, lowering her eyes.

"Then you are afraid of the Ancient One?" Deetra asked.

The girl did not answer and did not look up.

The others, except Tolar, also lowered their eyes.

They were all afraid, except Tolar.

How did it happen?

How did the fear begin?

Deetra looked to the man Tolar who dared to think of Hanta and began to tell him of her first memories of the Great One; how she held him in awe and feared him; how that fear changed to trust and love when she had yielded to him; and how he had guided and protected her when she was lured into dangerous adventures in the inbetween worlds.

"You are not afraid of Hanta?" Tolar asked Deetra.

The others, including Geta, looked up to see her answer.

"No," Deetra said, smiling. "I love Hanta. He is my dearest friend."

"How dare you say that!" Geta shot back.

"I do dare because it is the truth," Deetra said softly. "I cannot fear Hanta and, if you do, you must also fear me."

"Why should we fear you?" Geta asked suspiciously.

"Because I don't fear Hanta, and because I am, in a sense, his messenger."

"Then I do fear you," Geta said.

"I don't," Tolar said, defending her. "I don't fear you at all. I trust you."

"Thank you."

"And so do I," another said.

"And I."

"And I," the others chimed in.

[*16*]

Geta folded her arms tightly across her chest and lowered her eyes as if listening.

"I will leave you with one very important lesson," Deetra said earnestly. "Think about what has happened here today and, when you think, try to realize that when you think of someone or something you are in touch with that person or thing. What you feel in your imagery is what you convey in message to that person or thing." Deetra rose to her feet. "That is all for today," she said. "We will discuss your experiences on this matter at our next meeting."

Deetra turned and walked off, leaving her students where she had met with them. It was early in the day. There was time to visit her father's house and to catch up on family matters. She had not seen Starn, her father, for some time and, as always when she missed him, she had been talking with him in her thoughts, tuning in telepathically.

"May I walk with you?" a voice asked hesitantly from behind.

Deetra turned. Tolar waited respectfully.

"If you are going my way, you may," Deetra said lightly.

"I am and I'd like to," Tolar answered.

They moved on silently for a few moments. Deetra could hear the anxiety in the man's mind, scattered questions that really were not questions at all. She knew the man was hungry and impatient for knowledge.

"I wonder if you would mind if," he hesitated, searching for the proper words.

"No, Tolar, I would not mind you asking me anything. Please feel free to do so."

"Awakening Day is not for a hundred years," he said anxiously.

"Yes, that's right, Tolar."

"But do I have to wait that long. It could be another lifetime for me to ... to .... "

Deetra stopped walking and turned to the man. She

knew what he was suffering. The others in the class were relieved by the distant future of Awakening Day, whereas Tolar was painfully impassioned by its distance.

"Where were you this past Awakening Day?" Deetra asked.

"My wife was dying. I could not leave her," Tolar said softly. "she wanted me to go and seek my way, but I could not leave her."

Deetra continued walking again. "I see," she said thoughtfully, "and how did you intend to seek your way if you had left her?"

"I had many schemes," Tolar said. "I had thought of approaching the Elders for assistance and I had even thought of journeying to Moonwalk to ask the Hanta directly."

Deetra glanced at her companion and quickly turned her head away again. She doubted whether it would have done any good to approach the Elders, and to approach Moonwalk at a time when it was forbidden ground to the villagers could have been disastrous. She herself had been invited as the others with her had been. She was given a crystal as a tool to learn with, and, most important, she was under the protection of Hanta.

"Tolar, did it occur to you that if you were meant to participate in this past Awakening Day that you would have been invited to do so?"

"Yes. Yes it did, but I couldn't accept it."

"And why could you not accept it?"

"I don't know."

Tolar walked quietly beside her. The frustration nagged within him and he could not hide it. "I'm not good enough, I guess."

"I doubt that!" Deetra said, stopping and lightly touching the man on his arm. "See if you can understand what I am about to say."

"I will try," the man said. He could feel the tears swell

in his eyes and the display of emotion embarrassed him. He looked away momentarily, wondering if Deetra's touch had created it, releasing the pent up feelings within him.

"In the material world in which we live, we are bound by time. It requires time for this, and time for that, and everything that requires time has its own time, individually for everything as well as for each of us. Do you understand?"

Tolar nodded attentively, not sure that he did.

"Then you must also understand," she continued, "that my time is not necessarily your time. You were attending to a dying wife. You could not have left her in good conscience, so you were not invited to do so. Your place was with her, not on Moonwalk."

"But how can I be sure I did not miss my moment in time?"

"You can be sure," Deetra answered. "The only way you can miss your moment in time is by personal choice."

"But staying with my wife was choice."

"Was it?" Deetra paused and began walking again, this time more slowly for her companion's sake.

"I see," Tolar said. "My choice was to be with Hanta, but my responsibility held me back."

"That is correct. The Master will never interfere with our responsibilities. After all, they were once born out of choice. You gave your love to your wife and accepted the responsibility of caring for her. Now if you could have done both, that would have been acceptable. It could work. You see, making the choice to serve Hanta is a great responsibility. Now you have the opportunity to put your spiritual life first; before you couldn't."

"You mean I must never marry again?"

"No, I don't mean that. I am about to marry, but my personal life is secondary to the spiritual. It depends on your priorities and how you view them."

Tolar grew deeply thoughtful and did not speak again

for a long while. They walked silently. Deetra turned her attention elsewhere, to her father's house which was just around the corner. As they approached, she stopped, again touching Tolar lightly on the arm.

"I must leave you now," she said. "I hope our little talk has helped somewhat."

"It has."

"Good. As for your spiritual progress, ask Hanta to help you."

The man appeared stunned by her last statement. Deetra smiled at him, turned, and headed down the road around the corner toward her father's house. He stood looking after her, wondering at what sort of being she was.

How could he ask Hanta for help?

In deed?

In thought?

How?

As Deetra entered her father's house she could still feel Tolar's presence and hear the question she had risen in the man's mind. She knew he would find his way to Hanta and into Hanta's heart, as she had done, if he truly wanted it. She could only encourage him, nothing more; but yet, how exciting it was to participate in some small way in Tolar's great adventure. How wonderful it was to be a channel for the Divine Force.

She was so lost in thought she did not hear her father enter from behind.

"Well, my beautiful daughter, you have come!"

Deetra swung about and threw her arms about her father's neck. He hugged her back and then gently broke the hold. "Let me look at you," he said.

Deetra smiled, laughing lightly as the feeling of being a child again rushed to her. "Well, how do I look?" she asked, playfully.

Starn laughed, then grew serious, looking at her. "You look older, more mature, more like a woman about to marry."

"Oh father, and how does a woman about to marry look?"

"Beautiful. But the beauty has a special quality to it, a giving quality," he said softly, as if remembering.

Deetra caught the soft, flowing impression of another woman. "You are thinking of my mother," she said. "Do I remind you of her?"

"Just before we were to marry your mother looked as you do now. These physical bodies we're wearing may be just a lump of clay but they have the ability to radiate light through joy. The joy is produced through love."

Deetra studied the tenderness on her father's face. His firm, strong features glowed with a softness. She had seen it in him before, but never had she seen him direct his attention this way to her.

"How is Ian?" he asked.

"He sends you his fondest greetings."

Starn's expression sobered.

"Do you know why you are here today?" Starn asked.

"I know that I was drawn to visit you today," Deetra said. "And I can feel that you are about to tell me why." She smiled, waiting.

"From our conversation, surely you can guess," Starn said.

Deetra studied his expression again. Their conversation had been about Deetra's rise to womanhood, about marriage. She gripped the thought, enduring the bittersweet pain that swelled within her. She loved Ian next to God and she wanted to marry him but .... No, she must look at it, but what?

"Tell me of your love for Ian."

Deetra could feel the blood drain from her face. Starn knew exactly what she felt. It was why he had called on her telepathically to visit.

"Tell me," Starn asked again.

[*21*]

"I love him with all my heart," she said, pausing.

"And?" he asked.

"And I fear .... " She stopped. What she was saying made little sense to her.

"What do you fear?" Starn prodded.

"That I am not big enough."

"In what way?"

Deetra reflected on the questioning her father was giving her, and it reminded her of her village class just an hour before. Those present, except Tolar, had been afraid of Hanta, of his *being*. Now she was reflecting their circumstances, or was it the other way around. She was the teacher. How well she knew that a student could only rise as high as his teacher. She was afraid. She was the carrier of that fear. Her students were reflecting her. If they were to move on she would first have to face her fears and leave them behind.

"Let us return to the root of your fear," Starn said.

He had heard her thoughts.

"The razor's edge is very fine when I am with Ian," she said quietly.

"I can imagine. And I can imagine Ian's feelings toward the razor's edge," Starn said.

"What do you mean?" Deetra asked.

"Ian has spent many years caring for the physical needs of the Silent One."

"And now Ian carries that greatness with him," Deetra added. "Sometimes...." She stopped herself. The sound current shrieked in her inner ear like a warning. Then it leveled into a gentle melody again. She looked deeply into Starn.

He had witnessed her warning as well.

"Sharing a life with one spiritually advanced is a great opportunity, and it is also a great responsibility. Perhaps it is the latter that you fear, my daughter."

Yes. It was the responsibility she feared, and yet it

was the responsibility that gave meaning to her life. It was the life of one who was living to be a channel for the Divine Force. Hanta had asked her if she was prepared and she had answered him yes. Why now did she hesitate?

"It is easy to accept responsibility in words," Starn said, speaking her thought. "Now the time for action has come. You may make the choice again—to accept or reject the responsibility. You do not have to marry Ian."

Life without Ian! Deetra could not imagine it. She loved him. As friends and companions they shared everything. What would life be like without their union?

Impossible.

There could be no other for her.

She could not live alone among the villagers and be happy.

Without happiness, without joy, she could not serve as a Divine Channel.

What could she do?

She laughed at the ridiculous questioning her mind prompted. Starn knew her feelings and laughed with her.

"I will be happy to marry my love Ian at the proper time," Deetra said earnestly.

Starn sobered. "The proper time is now," he said, studying his daughter, catching her by the hand.

She stared at him blankly, off guard, then laughed at herself again. "Then it is now," she said.

"Then you accept the responsibility?" he asked.

"Yes," she said. "When is the date?"

"At the new moon."

Deetra could not believe what she heard. The new moon was only three days away. There was almost no time for preparation.

"It is Hanta's request. Sarpent has sent the message to me," Starn said.

Deetra looked deeply into her father. There was an air of excitement in his eyes, and there was something else.

He seemed to know something that he hadn't told her. Whatever it was he had been careful not to think an image or spark a feeling about it, and Deetra could not tell what it was.

"Does Ian know of our marriage date?" she asked her father.

"I'm sure he does," Starn said carefully. "He has been summoned to Hanta's sanctuary, so Sarpent told me."

"Did Sarpent tell you more?" Deetra asked.

Starn lowered his eyes, turned about, and began to hum a tune. Within a moment, the excitement had left his countenance. He turned back to face Deetra. "You will stay here tonight my daughter. In the morning, you will seek our Sarpent and find out the plan for your preparation."

Tolar stood in the doorway of the sanctuary, deeply hesitant. Suppose no one would help him. He had searched for Hanta and had not found him. If the Elders turned him away now, he would not know where to search next. Tolar immediately cut the thought off. They would help him. They were holy men. It was their duty to help him. him.

He knocked on the heavy wooden door and stepped back.

There was no answer.

He reached forward and knocked again, this time harder, more bold.

No answer.

He knocked again.

Again, no answer.

Tolar stood looking at the door for a long while, wondering if the door was about to open. Then he did a bold thing. He reached forward and pushed the door open. He entered.

He stood completely alone in a most peculiar surroundings filled with a brilliant blue light. The light was all he could see. It filled every inch of space, crowding it, moving around and through him.

What had he done?

Where was he?

He could feel the cold thrill of fear rippling down his spine and, in an effort to control himself, he let out a cry: "Is anyone there?"

The blue light was suddenly alive, throbbing, moving deeply into him and speaking, but he could not hear what it was saying. The fear held him. It was unbearable, painful, and, in a sudden gripping agony, he fell to the floor unconscious.

Gradually Tolar opened his eyes. He was lying on the cold stone floor just inside the sanctuary. The blue light was gone. How long had he been there? Had no one heard his knock or responded to his intrusion? The door had not been locked and so he had entered. Slowly, he raised himself to his feet and looked about.

He stood in the center of a stone room. There was really nothing to see—stone floor, stone walls, and no decoration of any kind. The doorway through which he had entered seemed to be the only opening and that led back into the world from which he had come. It appeared that the room was used for nothing; that no one ever came there.

Why was it there?

Why a doorway leading nowhere?

What of the blue light? Had he imagined it?

Where would he go to find Hanta now?

These things rang through Tolar's mind. He had a feeling of mounting panic. He remembered his fear upon entering the room; how it had overcome him; and how he awakened from it to find nothing. Was it always nothing or had his fear created nothing? He didn't know why, but he sensed that there was more, only his fear had made it invisible to him.

Why had he been afraid?

The blue light!

What was it?

In his uncertainty, Tolar called on Hanta and began to speak aloud. He told Hanta of his desire to awaken within the inner circle, to become conscious of all spiritual law; to share in the responsibility of being a channel for the Divine Force, and he offered his life to the Great One in exchange.

The stone walls stood stoically, not responding to the outpouring of the man's heart, or so it seemed. The wish stood cold, echoing back at him like rejection. Aware of a soft desperate cry within himself, Tolar turned on his heels and calmly walked toward the door. Suddenly, he stopped surprised.

Rian stood in the doorway. He had heard the man's speech and felt a great compassion for him. "Welcome to the place where Hanta rests," he said softly, extending a hand in welcome to the man.

Tolar took the young man's hand but said nothing.

"My name is Rian. I am the scribe, charged with copying the scriptures." He hesitated, aware that the older man was deeply disturbed. "If you would care to rest in my apartment, I would be happy to take you there."

Tolar, still surprised by the young man's sudden appearance, took his invitation as an omen and was hopeful. "Yes," he said, "I would like that very much."

Rian entered the stone room and casually went to a door in the opposite wall and opened it, beckoning his guest to follow.

Tolar hesitated, bewildered. What had seemed to be blank stone wall contained a door, which he could now see plainly.

He had been right!

Fear had blinded him. The door had been there all along.

Rian led the man down a long dimly lit corridor that opened into a courtyard. Flowers of every color grew there and among them were hummingbirds and golden bees, alive in the afternoon sunlight.

Tolar hesitated, taking in the glorious sight.

"My apartment is just on the other side," Rian said, noting the rapture on his companion's face. "It is a lovely place to take up residence."

"Indeed it is," Tolar said quickly. "You must be very special in the eyes of the Hanta to live in such a special place."

Rian studied the man absently. He had never thought of himself as special in Hanta's eyes. The man's observation was taken as a compliment. "Thank you," he said, motioning the man to follow.

They crossed the courtyard and entered a door. The apartment was large and airy, filled with light and color as the courtyard had been. On the floor against one wall were several sitting rugs, next to them a large window with a view that encompassed the mountains and the forest. To the right of them was a long wooden table, a chair, and shelves upon shelves stacked with scrolls.

"I can see you are very busy," Tolar said, trying to notice every detail.

"It's not a task to ever finish," Rian said, smiling. "It will take lifetimes, into the distant future, forever perhaps...." He stopped, catching himself wandering aimlessly in that direction. "Yes, it is a very pleasant apartment," he said again.

"My name is Tolar," the man said.

"Yes, I know. I heard you speaking in the entranceway."

"Then you know why I am here."

"Yes."

"Will you help me?" Tolar asked.

"In what way?"

Rian sat on the sprawl of colorful sitting rugs and indicated for the man to join him, knowing well what his visitor was asking, yet seeking time to prepare an answer. He did not feel he had access to Hanta.

"Take me to Hanta," Tolar said, firmly in a pleading tone.

"Each person must meet the Hanta on his own, in his own time," Rian paused, unsure of how to convince the man. "Don't you have a teacher in the village who can explain?"

"Yes, I have a teacher. She told me just hours ago to seek the Hanta and ask for his help. I am doing just that," Tolar said impatiently.

"Perhaps your teacher meant you to seek him inwardly and to ask for guidance at that inner temple," Rian said, catching a glimpse of Deetra from the man's mind. "Who is your teacher?" he asked, hoping to learn more of her.

"The Lady Deetra," Tolar said.

"And what else did she say?" Rian asked, probing.

"She said Hanta was not to be feared but to be considered a guide and a friend."

Rian looked deeply into the man's mind as he spoke, easily seeing the vision of Deetra telling her class about love and friendship with the Ancient One. It was her way and Rian had always been somewhat envious of her for it. She did love the Hanta openly and without reservations of any kind, whereas Rian was still trying to feel that closeness with the Master.

"I will do as I can," Rian said finally, rubbing his hands together as if to warm himself. "I am only the scribe here . . . ." He stopped. Tolar was looking at him curiously.

"You do not want to help me?" Tolar said.

Rian noted the determination on the man's face, prepared for Rian's denial of help. How could he say yes? How could he say no? The peculiar circumstances made it impossible for him to think. "Yes, I do want to help you," Rian said earnestly, "and I will do what I can."

Tolar relaxed, reaching out his hand in gratitude. "Thank you," he said, "thank you with all my life."

Rian rose from his seat.

Tolar jumped to his feet next to him.

Rian stared at the man in disbelief, realizing that he was expected to suddenly produce the Hanta's physical presence. "I will do what I can," he said, "but you will have to wait outside."

Rian led the way back into the courtyard, throught the dimly lit corridor, and returned Tolar to the stone entranceway where he had found him. "If you will wait here," he said, "I will see what I can do for you."

He left.

Tolar was suddenly struck with terror, looking about at the grey stone walls, watching as Rian retreated back inside the corridor, closing the door behind him. The door was instantly invisible, as it had been before Rian had appeared.

Why was it not visible to him?

Was he mad?

Had fear once again blinded him?

Tolar tried to calm himself, to move slowly around the solid stone walls in search of the door, but the more he tried the harder his heart pounded. It tore at him from within his chest like a giant drum, growing increasingly louder until he felt that his body would burst from the intensity of the sound. Unable to take command of himself any longer, he turned, ran for the open door that led back to the village, and bolted through it.

Rian paused in the corridor. He felt an unusual sensation, a sensation of panic. He grew calm within himself, wondering at the feeling. Then he thought of Tolar, how strangely the man had acted, and he realized that the man had run away, that he was no longer waiting for him in the entranceway.

CHAPTER 3

Deetra awoke suddenly, her father gently shaking her from a sound sleep. She looked up at him questioningly.

"You have a visitor, a messenger from Hanta," he said softly.

She quickly arose, leaving her sleeping mat and wrapping a robe about herself. There was a peculiar dream-like quality to her movements and, as she became aware of them, it seemed that the action was part of a dream. She hesitated, looking blankly into space as if trying to check on herself.

"Look alive, my daughter," Starn said seriously, taking his daughter by the arm. He had heard her inner confusion. "He awaits you outside."

Deetra hurried through the doorway and stepped outside. An old man, seemingly as old as Hanta, stood before her with a calm but urgent expression.

He bowed.

Courteously, Deetra bowed back, and as she did so she looked up. The face was not the face of the old man at all, but the face of Ian smiling sweetly at her. She was too astonished to speak.

Was she asleep?

Had her dream infiltrated her waking state?

Who was he?

"My Lord Hanta asks that the preparations for your wedding be kept simple, yet public." He paused, studying her to see if she was paying attention, then continued: "All the village will be witness to your wedding, which will be held at dawn of the new moon. Even now they are being told of the news."

Ian was no longer there. The old man returned to the countenance before her. He continued: "The Eastern tribes will be in attendance as well. Lord Casmir has already been notified."

Deetra wondered why her marriage was of importance to so many.

The messenger grew very still, looking deeply into her. As he did, Deetra saw an image of Hanta, only the face was not the face of Hanta at all. It was the face of someone else, turning toward her. It was Ian.

Confused, she looked away, asking with half-turned head: "What is it that Hanta wishes me to do?"

"To prepare yourself through contemplation," the old man answered, "the rest will be taken care of for you, even to your wedding robes and the reception following."

Deetra looked up, surprised.

"That is the message," the old man said.

"And do I wait here until the day? Do I stay with my father?" she asked hopefully.

"You are to come with me now," the man said. "Hanta has prepared quarters for you."

Deetra knew better than to argue or try to change the plan, it was just that she couldn't understand her surprise. Why was it she had not known; not heard within the inner planes what was to become of her. She had grown so accustomed to being tuned in on matters concerning herself that she found it difficult to accept that a major plan had been formed without her knowledge. She wondered if Ian had known or had been surprised as well. Then she remembered the expression on his face when she had interrupted his contemplation just before Casmir's arrival. He seemed to be realizing something that didn't concern her at the time. At least she asked him no questons, believing that he would share with her anything that related to her being.

She turned about, hoping to see her father there, but he was within the house. Then she turned back to the old man again. "I will be ready shortly," she said. "Please be comfortable until then."

She went into the house.

The journey to the sanctuary was swift. The old man offered her no conversation and the only impression she could lift from his mind was a faceless countenance of Hanta. She focused in on that image, disciplining her mind to be still on it, knowing full well that she would soon be told all. There was little need for her to concern herself with details now. The messenger, she was sure, had told her all that she was to be told, or perhaps all that he knew. She would have to wait, in mental silence, while they hurried along the road.

They arrived at the rear entrance of the sanctuary. The old man pushed the heavy wooden door open and motioned her to enter. Then he hurried across the plain stone room and opened another door, leading up a long dimly lit corridor and stepped within the beautiful sunlight of the courtyard. Deetra paused to admire it and was quickly hurried on her way again by the old man. As she moved behind him, she thought of Rian and wondered where she would find the scribe, remembering fondly their many adventures through the *inbetween worlds*.

The old man paused and turned to Deetra. "The scribe's residence is at the end of the courtyard," he said, speaking her thought.

"Thank you," she said.

They hurried on, winding from corridor to corridor, stopping finally at an entranceway guarded by an iron gate. Beyond it, the light faded, gradually becoming extreme darkness.

"You must go through the gate alone," the old man said. "It is where Hanta has said he will meet with you." Then he turned and hurried off in the direction they had come.

Deetra paused before the gate, feeling the mighty presence of the Silent One, then entered unafraid. Since it was dark, she saw with her inner eyes, trusting herself, yielding to the divine life force and flowing with it, through the intense blackness. It seemed to go on, then suddenly the darkness turned to light, supreme intense light, and there in the middle of it stood the Ancient One, beckoning her to him.

Slowly, or so it seemed in the intense light, Deetra approached. She could see him and yet she couldn't, the details of his face were defused. She moved seemingly without movement. He extended a hand to her and she reached out to take it. Suddenly, as their fingers interlocked, she was no longer outside the light and blinded by it, but within the light, and the form who held her hand was plainly visible.

She thought that her heart had stopped.

It was Ian!

Suddenly, Ian's face became the Ancient One's again. It was Hanta or was it? She remembered a time long ago when she had first been given a crystal as a tool to view life; how, sitting under an old oak in the fields near her father's house, she had looked through the crystal and had seen Ian, and how that image of Ian had turned into the image of Hanta.

What did it mean?

She released the thought and let her mind grow still

and blank, focusing her total being on the spiritual eye just between the eyebrows. It was then that she heard the Ancient One speak.

"I am a consciousness and that consciousness's name is Hanta. I infuse myself into a human form that can and will accept the responsibility of leading souls through the psychic worlds. My life then becomes all lives, and as I teach and guide those who wish to follow me to Awakening Day, my identity becomes infused with their identity. We become One.

"When the human form I use has been exhausted or when I wish the change of human form, I begin to seriously look about to see which of my followers is ready and willing to accept the responsibility of accepting the Hanta consciousness. I cannot choose the female form because it lacks the chemical battery, the physical strength to assume the power, and, although a woman can gain mastership of the detached state or higher consciousness, her form cannot sustain the intense electrical-like current that must pass through the vehicle. She would be literally burned to death. And so I must prime a man for the task, one who is pure of heart and willing to accept the burden.

"The choice is few. Many are primed for the task, but only one succeeds."

The Ancient One paused, turned away, and when he turned back again, he was Ian.

Deetra was too astonished to speak.

Ian smiled sweetly at her.

"Is it you?" she asked finally.

"Now that you know, you must again ask yourself if you wish to share my life in marriage. Bear in mind that you would be living within the Hanta's light; that you would be loved by some and feared by many. Our relationship would be of the highest of unions, but also of the highest responsibility." He stopped, looking deeply into her, knowing full well that her answer was not possible at this time.

Deetra needed time to be alone.

"Leave me and find your peace, Beloved. We will meet again when you are ready," Ian said. Then he tenderly kissed her hand and held it to his cheek. "I love you Deetra and, should you wish to be my wife, I will be exceedingly joyful. Go now. A room has been prepared for you in which to be alone and decide."

He released her hand.

Numbly, Deetra turned about and exited back through the darkness, through the iron gate. On the outside the old messenger waited to take her to her chamber.

Deetra sat alone in the lovely chamber that had been prepared for her. Although it was brilliantly lit and colorful with various shades of blues and yellows and white, and bowls of fresh-cut flowers placed about, her heart was dark and heavy. She felt the terrible shock of her lover transformed into the untouchable being. Yet he had touched her as a lover would touch. And who was to say that the Hanta was not also a man? He was a mystical consciousness, spiritual consciousness, but the body and mind were composed of the same matter as any man. He could laugh or cry like any man. He ate when he was hungry like any man. Ian was still Ian, the man she loved with all her heart, the man with whom she wished to share life.

Deetra moved about the room restlessly. She knew why the chamber had been prepared for her. She could not move among the other Askans without having her thoughts known. She recalled how, long ago when she and Rian and Curtser were on their journey to the City of Light, they had become aware of the universal mind and had gradually developed the awareness to look into the minds of people and things. It was how they had learned discrimination. They had also learned the great power of thought; how it could build or destroy; how it could change things from one form to another. But the greatest awareness of all was the recognition of the perceiver of mind, the perceiver of feelings and of sight and sound—Soul.

Looking back through the experiences that led to the awareness she now had, Deetra was amazed at the distance she had travelled. On one hand, there was no distance at all but, on the other, it was greater than the vast heavens in the sky. The difference was the difficult part to believe. She had always known everything, *but* she had not been aware of what she knew. Deetra reflected on her position now. She had come to the point where she recognized Soul and was developing control over mind, but what great adventures must assuredly be awaiting her? Would she stop here where she was comfortable? No, she could not do that. She had to go on, to continue that great adventure toward total awareness.

Deetra sat down on the plush pale-blue cushion built up against the wall and, for the first time, admired the splendor of the room. It was by far the most elegant setting she had ever seen. The cloths were finely spun silks and the decorations about the chamber were ornaments of gold and silver and precious jewels. The area sparkled and glistened and, looking up, Deetra saw why.

The ceiling was not a ceiling at all. Seemingly, it was open sky and brilliant sunlight. But how could this be? Then she saw a clear substance serving as a ceiling. How wonderful! The entire chamber was alive with light and color, and yet protected from the elements. How could she not have seen such a spectacle on first entering the room? She chuckled to herself, remembering the heaviness she was experiencing when first she entered. Life in her heart was not darkened any longer.

She thought of Ian, of how they had first met in the marketplace, he telling her that it was all right for her to question the meaning of Awakening Day. Their relationship began strangely and yet it was not really strange. She had been spurred by inner turmoil and question, and unknowingly she carried these feelings in her aura. Ian simply picked up on them. He was in service to the Hanta, but he was also a man. He had assisted her many times during her journey to the City of Light and he had come to admire her willingness to learn. She was aware of this admiration and it was mutual. She grew to trust him and enjoy him. She wanted to be near him, to touch him. They were friends as well as lovers. Yes, the human feelings were real and there was complete freedom in the feelings. They did not restrict one another by possession or negative thought. They allowed each other to *be* and shared their *beingness,* and she knew for both of them that Soul perceived this happiness.

Her goal was to become master of herself and to realize the ultimate of God. If he was Hanta he would comfort her just as she would comfort him. The untold responsibility he had accepted would seem much less a burden with a friend at his side. As for herself, the opportunity, not only for awareness but for love, with Ian as her partner in life was limitless.

The answer was YES.

Of course she would marry Ian!

It was as though her silent answer had been shouted. There came a change in the chamber, an immediate change in mood and intensity but something else. A peculiar pungent odor filled the room. Deetra was aware that some unseen forces were at work but she could not identify them until gradually she saw that there was form manifesting.

She watched.

A tall, strongly built man in a maroon tunic appeared before her, smiling. He had the eyes of Hanta, deep and piercing, but his manner of dress and speech showed him to be of another land.

"My name is Malitara Tatz," he said matter-of-factly, taking a seat on the cushion next to her. "It is my intention to be your guide on the journey to God-Realization."

Deetra stared at the strong features of his bearded face, too astonished to speak.

"Your marriage to Ian will require a guiding hand. Living on the outside of the light, reaching in, is one matter and living on the inside is quite another. Do you understand?"

"I think I do," Deetra said, somewhat meekly. "But who are you?"

"I have told you my name," the man said.

"But," she said, starting to protest, then caught herself.

The bearded man smiled. "It is not true that all Hantas die when they leave the job," he said. "I stepped away after many, many years of service to shift the title to another part of the world. In other words, I trained a successor in your land and so the line of succession has continued here until it is time to move the seat of power again." He paused, deeply studying her. "Do I make myself clear?"

"Yes," Deetra answered enthusiastically. "And I am so happy to hear that all Hantas do not have to die after Awakening Day."

Malitara Tatz laughed. "There are many myths among the people," he said, "and I see there are also many among the Askan. But there is plenty of time to teach you these things. For now, we have met. I will return at another time."

"But on what occasion?" Deetra asked.

"On the right occasion," Malitara Tatz said, smiling. "We will meet again."

As soon as the man called Malitara Tatz had disappeared, there was a knock at her chamber door.

The door opened.

Sarpent stepped into the room and bowed slightly in greeting.

Deetra rose to her feet.

"Hanta has asked that I prepare you and Ian for your marriage," Sarpent said, turning to wave the servants behind him to enter. They were carrying bundles of things. "There

[*38*]

are but a few hours left. I will check on you later," Sarpent said. "The servants will help you dress."

Sarpent looked hard at the girl, turned, and left.

Deetra looked after him, remembering the uncomfortable look in his eyes and his opening words. He said *Hanta had asked* him to prepare her and Ian. Then he did not know. She quickly put a clamp on her thoughts, gazing about at the servants to see if they had seen into her, but the servants were busily unwrapping the coil of fine silk.

A large tub was brought in and the servants filled it with water, crushing flower petals into it for their fine scent, and motioned her to enter.

She stepped into the tub and submerged herself, yielding to the knowing hands of the servants who rubbed the flower petals over her skin and into her hair. Then they dried her, wrapped her in a warm robe, and brought her some tea.

Deetra sat on the floor cushions, silently sipping her tea, watching as the servants had the tub removed from her chamber, and returned checking and rechecking the folds of her wedding dress, which they had laid out on the floor at the other end of the room. The scent of flowers was strong, and the strength of the scent reminded her of the scent that had filled the room when Malitara Tatz had appeared. It was distinctly different however, a strong woodsy scent and nothing quite like any she had ever known. And she remembered too the imposing features of her visitor's face. Quickly she checked her thoughts again and looked to see if the servants had picked up on them. No one seemed to notice but, hurrying about, they motioned her to stand. It was time to dress.

The dress was pale gold and it draped her body perfectly, gracefully falling to the floor in long pleats. They straightened it and restraightened it on her body, checking themselves and her in remembering details of Sarpent's orders. Finally, they stood back from Deetra and studied her admiringly.

"You have done well," Deetra told them.

They nodded appreciatively, bowed, and left the room. At their exit the door opened again. Sarpent entered, eyed the girl, then turned and stood back from the door, bowing slightly at the entranceway.

The Ancient One entered.

Deetra lifted her eyes to meet his. All the love of her life poured forth to greet him. It was he who guided and protected her to the City of Light, who accepted her as an Askan and raised her in consciousness, and it was he who blessed her union with Ian.

At a certain impulse Sarpent left the chamber.

The Ancient One extended his hand to her. Deetra reached to take it. As their hands met an incredible change occurred. The Ancient One was no longer the Hanta. It was Ian and in his inner communication with her he explained that no one but herself was yet aware of what had transformed; that he had merged with the Ancient One until such time that his new identity as Hanta could be established in the communities at large.

Deetra was not surprised. She had known that he had accepted the responsibility of Hanta, but she had not understood that he had merged with the Ancient One. Then she told him of her visitor Malitara Tatz.

Ian smiled warmly. "He is my good friend, Deetra, and now he will be yours as well. He is one of the great masters who assist the Hanta in the spiritual guidance of the world. Trust him completely, as I do."

"I will," Deetra said. "But, dearest, do tell me where he is from. His dress and manner are so unusual and there is a thick wood-scent about him."

"You will always know he is near if the scent is near," Ian told her." The Master Tatz lives in a country called Tibet, in a spot so remote, high in the mountains, that the air is thin and difficult to breathe."

"Have you been there?" she asked.

"Yes, and so shall you someday," Ian said, "but now we must prepare for our wedding."

It was then that Deetra noticed the same pale gold silk adorning Ian's form as her own. "You look very wonderful," she said.

"As do you, beloved," he answered. "Let us be on our way so that we may walk slowly hand-in-hand to the platform at Bell Rock where we are to marry."

The wedding procession formed outside the sanctuary walls in the early morning darkness. There all the Elders gathered, including Sarpent who took the lead. "Come, prepare yourselves," he called loudly. "We must be on our way."

Ian and Deetra took their place directly behind Sarpent and waited quietly until the others were properly assembled and Sarpent gave the command. Then they walked on slowly, keeping pace with the leader.

The chill of the night air seemed to sing to them as they moved through it. The sound was radiant and pure and, listening to it, Deetra was sure it was singing HUuuuu.

"It is the ancient name for God," Ian whispered, aware of her thoughts. "The name is HU, and it is sung HUuuuu."

She turned to him, gazing into the soft warm glow of his deepset blue eyes. Never had he looked more wonderful.

Ian smiled lovingly at her. "Listen," he said softly. "The HUuuuu is our escort."

Deetra marveled at the sound. It was like all other sounds of silence she had heard and yet now her perception of it was so clear there was no mistaking the HU. She thought of the many times the sound in its various forms had led her. She had grown accustomed to its presence. It was the sound current of all sounds, and she had grown to live with it constantly and to depend upon its presence.

Sarpent moved easily through the semi-darkness, quickening his step as they neared Bell Rock. The dawn was fast-approaching now and they were still a short distance away. They moved more quickly behind him.

The platform was beautifully prepared with garlands of flowers. Those to be in attendance were already gathered. There were people from villages everywhere, a representative from each formed a large semi-circle at the back of the platform. The others stood quietly below, watching as the wedding procession ascended the stone steps and took their places on the platform. It was then, waiting with Ian in the center of the arena, that Deetra saw Rian. Their eyes met briefly as he was taking his place.

Sarpent stepped to the front of the platform, facing the large gathering below. "The Ancient One has requested that this marriage between Ian and Deetra be witnessed by all of you," Sarpent said, "and so it shall be!" He paused, looking up to the mountains and to the rising sun. Then he turned to Ian and Deetra. He stood gazing at them, waiting.

Gradually a thin streak of sunlight appeared, growing broader and bolder, overlapping the images of the marriage partners.

Sarpent waved his hand in a circle over Ian's and Deetra's heads. "May the blessings be!" he said.

"Blessed by the Hanta and witnessed by the villages of this land, you are now joined together, united in the bonds of marriage. You have chosen your union so that you may walk the spiritual path to God together. Make now your vow so that all may hear."

Ian and Deetra turned to face one another. They were smiling and love flowed from heart to heart. Ian nodded to his beloved to begin.

"I, Deetra, choose to merge my life with the life of Ian, to walk together with him on the spiritual path to God."

She looked lovingly into his eyes as she spoke, comfortable with the decision of her heart.

Then Ian spoke. The words were the same but something different was transpiring. As he spoke the ray of sunlight seemed to lift him, move through him, and when he reached out to take Deetra's hand he was alive with light and he took her into it with him. On the outside, nothing could be seen but the light. On the inside, they were as two beings joined together as one.

Gradually, the light subsided. Ian took Deetra by the hand and moved forward on the platform. Turning to his beloved once more, he kissed her lightly on the lips for all to see. As he did this the two were again wrapped in a globe of light.

A soft murmur went through the crowd.

Ian and Deetra separated again. This time they turned to Sarpent, Ian bowed lightly, catching a glimpse of recognition on the Chief Elder's face. Just as quickly, it disappeared. He knew, but then again he did not know.

"Go and be one with God," Sarpent said, completing the ceremony. Then he waved them on past him and watched as they disappeared at the rear of the platform.

The reception that followed was somewhat of a surprise to Deetra. Although the old messenger who brought her to the sanctuary had mentioned it in word, preparations had not been brought to her attention again. Now she stood with Ian in the glorious flowering courtyard within the sanctuary walls, surrounded by her father, friends, and well-wishing villagers. There would be a feast on the lawn later in the morning, but for now it was time to greet those who wished to share in their joy.

Starn embraced his daughter. "You are more beautiful this day than any in your life," he said, tenderly.

She started to thank him when someone touched her

shoulder from behind. She turned around.

It was Ian.

"I am needed elsewhere," he said gravely, "but I will return shortly. Treat our guests well."

Deetra tried to look into her husband but was cut off by a slight shake of his head. "I will return soon," he said again and, kissing her lightly, he turned and left the courtyard.

Starn squeezed his daughter's hand and motioned to a young man who was approaching. It was Rian and he carried a rolled parchment under his arm.

"How good it is to see you," Deetra said, extending her hand in greeting. "I have been wondering when we would meet again."

"And I as well," Rian said, smiling. "I recently met with a student of yours and he left in somewhat of a turmoil."

Deetra could easily see an image of Tolar as Rian spoke. "He came to you?" she asked.

"He came to find Hanta, and he happened on me," Rian said. "He seemed a desperate sort, begging me to help him to meet with the Great One." Then suddenly Rian terminated his thought and held up the parchment to Deetra. "A wedding present for you and Ian."

Deetra accepted the gift and started to break the seal that held the rolled parchment intact.

"Not here," Rian said, placing his hand over Deetra's on the parchment. "Wait until you and Ian are alone."

Deetra raised her eyes to meet Rian's. There was something mysterious about the gift and she was curious.

"Actually, it's more than a wedding gift," Rian said softly, "I am deeply puzzled by the contents and I need a friend to share it."

Deetra turned the rolled parchment about in her hand. It was new, perhaps a copy of scripture beautifully written by Rian's hand.

"Yes," he said nodding, "but there is more to it. Please wait."

The look on Rian's face cautioned Deetra and she tucked the parchment into a pocket in the folds of her gown, returning her attention to her friend. "Have you heard from Curtser?" she asked.

"No, have you?"

"Lord Casmir visited Ian. I was with him at the time and Casmir said that Curtser was well and sent his best regards."

"Is that all?" Rian asked.

"Precisely my words," she said, smiling. "Yes, that was all."

"And who is the Lord Casmir?" Rian asked, turning about to study the guests.

Across the courtyard, Starn was conversing with a tall, powerfully built man with dark skin and black hair. "He is there with my father," Deetra said.

"I know him," Rian said quickly.

"You do?"

"He looks strangely familiar to me," Rian said.

"And to me," Deetra said, studying the sharp lines of the man's face. "But I don't know where I've seen him."

Rian was quiet for what seemed a long while. "Could it have been on Moonwalk?" he asked thoughtfully.

Deetra looked up surprised. "He said that very thing to me."

"Who said?"

"Casmir said that perhaps we had met on Moonwalk, but I said that I didn't think so." Deetra stopped and turned to the bold man conversing now with her father. Who was he? A slow, cold chill ran through her as she asked, remembering how Ian had warned not to push information forward before its time. He had cautioned her that there was retribution for impatience, yet the feeling was distinct. Never before had she had the feeling that rushed through her now, except in the presence of one other. She turned. Rian was trembling at her side.

Looking back to Casmir again, she was certain.

They had met on Moonwalk.

It was the Pink Prince.

Deetra turned and gripped Rian's arm. His eyes met hers. "Yes," she said firmly, getting control of the feeling which rushed through her, "it is he in another form."

"But how?" Rian asked uncertain.

"I don't know, only that it is he."

"Does Starn know? Does anyone else know?" Rian asked.

Deetra looked to her father across the courtyard. He seemed somewhat ill at ease with Casmir but he gave no indication that he recognized the Lord from the East. Then she remembered how Ian had treated Casmir, the grave respect he had shown the visiting tribesman in spite of the man's manners regarding Hanta. Casmir had indicated that he was to be the next in line for the spiritual title. Ian had not opposed him.

Casmir looked across the courtyard at Deetra and Rian, drawn by the attention they were paying him.

Starn motioned her over from behind.

"What will we do?" Rian asked.

"Visit with the other guests, anything to shift your attention from Casmir. Pay him no more mind," she said. Then she hurried across the courtyard to her father.

Casmir greeted her fondly. "You make a beautiful bride," he said pleasantly.

"Thank you," she said, "and we are most honored to have a visitor from such a distant village."

"Hanta asked that I be here," Casmir said proudly.

Deetra bowed slightly, carefully guarding her thoughts. Then she reached for her father's hand. Turning to him, she asked, "Would you escort me to my chambers. I'd like to freshen up before the feast."

"Of course," Starn said and, excusing himself from Casmir's presence, he led his daughter around the back of the courtyard and through the narrow corridor that led to her private chamber.

When they were inside, Deetra asked if he had recognized Casmir.

"Wherever the positive force reigns, the negative is always present," Starn said seriously. "It is to be expected. No doubt the Lord Casmir will be a constant companion, preferred or not."

Deetra was struck by her father's words. What he said was true. The negative force would naturally follow the positive, only she had not thought on that matter before now.

"And you must not think on it now either," Starn said. "It is important that you carry out your duties this day without such thought. There will be time enough later to consider these matters."

"I understand," she said.

"Good. Then return to the reception as quickly as you can. I will leave you for a few moments." He kissed her on the cheek and squeezed her shoulders encouragingly. "You look very beautiful, my daughter," he said again, then he turned and left.

Deetra moved to the window, which opened on a brilliant green lawn. It was there the feast was to be held and the sanctuary servants scurried back and forth in preparation, carrying trays of vegetables and fruit and nuts to the long tables set up at the far end of the lawn. Several of the Elders directed them, shouting orders, not unpleasantly but with a keen excitement in their voices. As Deetra watched she thought of Ian, respecting his request by not wondering where he was but wishing to share with him her discovery of their Eastern visitor and her conversation with Rian.

But then, of course, he probably knew.

She remembered the parchment, feeling the bulge of

[47]

it in the pocket within the folds of her gown, and drew it out. Although Rian had said it was a wedding present and to open it with Ian, she did not wait. Without hesitation she slipped her thumbnail under the wax seal and broke it. The parchment unrolled before her eyes.

Written in Rian's hand she read:

THE MARK

The mark is that initiation which binds one to the inner master (or seat of consciousness within the worthy one). *It is the power, the wisdom, and the love bestowed upon those who have proven their readiness.*

The mark is visible to all who approach and yet its form is formless.

The presence of one who wears the mark is graceful with power, wisdom, and love (which is charity), *and all who approach recognize this.*

Recognition of a mark-wearer does not mean that he who recognizes will accept (without question or rebellion). *The rebellion may be fierce, such as the attraction of an opposing force.*

Those who wear the mark are the chosen ones and are protected by the positive forces (as long as opposing thought does not invade). *It is the responsibility of the mark-wearer to exercise control* (at all times).

(The mark, once placed, can never be removed.) *It is the heaven of he who serves the Divine Forces and the hell of he who finds he cannot.*

Deetra stared at the parchment, realizing with strange clarity that the gift Rian had given had been disturbing to him.

But why?

She studied the overall appearance of the parchment.

[*48*]

It was beautifully done, ivory colored with rich brown ink and the lettering was impeccable. Then she noticed that he had written in two different hands. What was within the brackets was written in a different hand than that which was written without.

How strange.

She recalled Rian's comment that there was more to the scroll than the words; that he had said he was deeply puzzled and needed a friend to share it.

A knock sounded at Deetra's chamber door. She rolled the parchment and returned it to the fold in her gown, then called, "Enter."

The door opened and the old messenger entered, bowing slightly. "My Lord Ian asks that you attend the feast without him. He regrets that he has been delayed and will join you as soon as he can."

"Thank you," Deetra said and, watching as the old messenger left, she marvelled at the striking clarity of the man who served Hanta so well.

The feast was a casual affair set on the rolling lawns just outside the sanctuary. There were hundreds in attendance and the great yard was alive with laughter and joy. Most were villagers and, although they moved with some uncertainty near the table where the Elders sat, they threw their inhibitions to the wind once out of their immediate company.

Music was heard everywhere. The tunes were those the villagers lived by, those they sang in work as well as celebration and joy.

Deetra loved the village music. It held such fond memories of her girlhood and now she could see how the songs were a foundation for Askan life. The tunes were simple as were the words but each held some small truth, which the consciousness could lean upon in difficult times.

She remembered the *Working Song* which she, Rian, and Curtser had sung on Moonwalk and how the tune had attracted Curtser's attention when he was frozen in a wall-less prison. Across the yard, a band of villagers danced in a circle with locked arms singing it:

Oh, a working day is play, is play when all the
farmers blend their hay and toil not to harsh a
day then oh, a working day is play, is play.

They sang the song over and over again, building in tempo until finally they switched to another.

Happiness is a spark, a spark of life that no one
can see, but oh, happiness is a spark, a spark
worn by all who wear the mark, the mark for all
to see.

The song was delightful to Deetra and her favorite although she had never stopped to analyze it. It said simply that happiness created a mark that was visible to others, or was that what it said?

She rolled the tune over again in her mind.

No. Happiness did not create the mark. The mark created happiness. Of course, how dense of her. It is exactly what the song says.

She reflected back to the parchment Rian had given her. Never had anyone or anything directly referred to the mark. Perhaps that was why she had never questioned the meaning of the song. But now the mystery grew in her. There was a mark and, when there was time, she would study the parchment and discuss it with Ian. Still, she couldn't help wondering why Rian had given it to her at this time, and why he would use two different forms of writing in the presentation of it.

It was then that Rian approached her. "I can see that you have read the parchment," he said, seriously.

"Yes, yes I have," Deetra answered thoughtfully.

"And what do you make of it?"

"I'm not sure," Deetra said. "It caught my attention

more strongly after listening to the *Happiness Song*."

Rian stepped back, lending an ear to the gaiety of the singing villagers. They were singing the *Happiness Song* and when they came to the word *mark* in the lyrics he turned back to Deetra. "I see what you mean," he said. "Oddly enough I hadn't caught that before."

"Nor had I," said Deetra.

There was a long silence between them, during which Deetra listened to the familiar music of the inner worlds. It was a pause that refreshed, a moment in which Soul soared within—fearless and limitless. Gradually, she became aware of her surroundings again.

Rian smiled, looking at Deetra. "The *force* is such a great friend," he said. "A moment away and nothing worldly visible is a surprise."

Deetra knew that he had enjoyed the music of the spheres as well. It was the mark of the Askan and she said this to him.

He nodded knowingly, then grew serious again. "It is not the meaning of the scroll that puzzles me," he said. "It is the manner in which it was written down."

Deetra studied the seriousness in Rian's face. She thought of the parchment and the way in which it was written. "You are referring to the two different handwritings," she said.

"Yes."

"Both are yours," she said again.

"On the parchment I gave you, yes. But on the original parchment, they are different. It is written by one person and added to by another. The other appears in the brackets as it does in the copy I gave you."

"And there is no explanation thereof?" she asked.

"None."

"Perhaps you had better discuss it with Ian," she said, turning her attention to the distant figure of a man approaching. Ian paused and waved to her, hurrying to where she stood with Rian.

They waited.

Ian met Deetra, lightly kissing her on the lips, and turned his attention to Rian who greeted him warmly. Then Deetra told Ian of the parchment Rian had given them as a gift, and Rian explained the question he was feeling.

"Where is the parchment now?" Ian asked.

"I gave the copy to Deetra," Rian said.

"It is here, in my gown pocket," Deetra said, patting her left side.

"Leave it there," Ian said. "Now is not the time for this matter." Then he dismissed Rian by saying that he would meet with him later.

Rian started to object, then paused, looking deeply into Ian's eyes. Something held him off, yet satisfied him. They would talk later. He bowed slightly and turned to leave them.

"It is time for us to celebrate with the others," Ian said. "Let us not forget that this is our wedding day." He took Deetra's hand and began to walk slowly through the gathering of villagers, warmly extending a hand in greeting as they passed.

When they had walked around the yard, Ian turned back to look at the people. "I'm glad our marriage feast is providing such a happy time," he said, gently squeezing Deetra's hand.

Deetra looked lovingly into Ian's eyes. She saw the sparkle of happiness there, but she also saw something else. In the Hanta consciousness of her husband there was a mysterious depth that she could not penetrate. As close as she was to Ian, she was outside of that part of him. It was a part that he could not share. That joy and that burden were for him alone.

Ian's attention was drawn to the Elder's table at the far end of the lawn. There Casmir was conversing with Sarpent. He seemed to be giving the Elder instructions, using his fingers to itemize some procedure or requests.

Deetra watched the scene with her husband.

Ian turned to her. "Let us leave now," he said. "Our duty is complete here."

CHAPTER 4

Rian stood before the black iron gate where the old messenger had left him, studying the depth of darkness beyond. He knew the Hanta waited within, yet never before had he been summoned to appear before him. It was a fate he had dreamed of, had wanted desperately but one which he also feared. The memory of his only meeting with the Ancient Ône stood nakedly in his mind. Why could he not forget; move forward to this present moment? Still he could see the Hanta handing him the crystal to launch his spiritual awakening and at the same time he could see the Ancient One turn his head as though he could not look at him.

Rian tried to calm the trembling that rose as the memory took form in his thoughts. Why was he so afraid? Was the fear a feeling of rejection or was it guilt? Guilt about what? No, rejection perhaps but not guilt. What reason would he have to feel guilty? He had done nothing, yet deep down inside he could not erase the feeling that he had done something. But what?

He looked deeply into the darkness that awaited him. Hanta was beyond. He thought of moving forward and entering but the trembling of his nerves made it seem impossible. He had to join the Master, but could not.

Then, as if some invisible companion comforted him, he grew calm. The calmness was sudden and in that instant he thought of Ian, of looking deeply into his eyes just before he and Deetra had left their wedding feast. There had been a flow between them, a feeling of sorts, filled with the depths of some remarkable knowingness. It was a comradeship and Rian knew that the matter of the scroll would come forward again at the right time. Perhaps this was the time.

Rian stepped easily into the darkness and followed it. At the end there was intense light and he lifted his eyes bravely to it.

The light was form, a form, and one that he recognized comfortably as Ian. But why was Ian the center of such intense light?

Ian did not speak but stood aglow as if at the edge of a great void. Then he did an astonishing thing. Ian was no longer Ian but the Ancient One. The form had transformed from one to the other. Rian looked deeper and was curiously unafraid. Ian returned to his sight, then the Ancient One again, then Ian, then the Ancient One again. Over and over this transformation happened, jumping from one image to the other. Finally it stopped. Ian stood with hand outstretched to Rian.

Rian took Ian's hand and was immediately drawn into the light. There he stood next to the husband of Deetra, curiously drawn but unafraid.

"I can see by your expression that you still do not know," Ian said softly.

Rian studied the strong features of the man next to him and he was filled with wonder.

Rian looked about. There was no visible space or object near them. It was as if Ian had been the center of the void and he, Rian, had joined him. Yes, he had taken his hand and joined him. He had entered the light. The light was the Ancient One's light. It was Hanta's light. Suddenly, it struck him and, as it did, Ian's form became that of the Ancient One's form and then returned to Ian's once more.

"Do you know who I am?" Ian asked.

"You are the Hanta," Rian answered, distantly as though in a dream. "You are the Hanta."

"You know," Ian said. Then anticipating his question, he said: "And I also bear the title of the Silent One, for in my role as Hanta, I am that also."

"And yet you speak."

"When you joined me within the light, you were able to hear the words of Soul. It is the secret way, the higher knowledge of the Askan. Do you understand?"

Rian nodded that he did and, as he looked into the face of Ian and saw the Hanta, his heart sang with joy. The Ancient One was eternal, the mantle of power passed from form to form. Rian thought his heart would burst with the discovery.

"The many questions that will come to you will be answered," Ian said softly, "but each in its own time."

Suddenly Rian was jolted to a memory of the Ancient One that he had carried with him to this meeting. Again his imagination clearly showed the Hanta turning his face away from him.

"You feel that you were rejected by the Master," Ian said, speaking his thoughts. "But in reality you were being accepted."

Rian looked deeply into Ian's eyes, trying to under-stand. A long moment passed and in it the memory that Rian held of receiving the crystal from Hanta changed to that of Hanta giving the crystal to Rian. It was as though Rian was not part of the scene but rather the observer and, as he watched the Hanta approach the young boy Rian in the fields where he worked, he saw the keen gleem of love pouring forth from the Ancient One's presence. The boy turned to meet the gaze of the Ancient One and, as he did, he called out "Help me! Help me!" Tears streamed down the boy's face and he was sobbing pitifully. The Ancient One stopped and, as the boy approached, he handed him a crystal, which the boy accepted but did not seem to see. Instead, he called out for help to the Ancient One again. The Hanta turned his head away from the boy and walked sorrowfully away.

"Did the Hanta reject the boy?" Ian asked, quietly breaking into Rian's vision.

Rian was still mesmerized by the scene. It was not quite as he had remembered it. In his memory his vision had been one dimensional; he had seen only from the boy's viewpoint and not the overview. His memory told him that the Master had turned away, rejecting him, but it was not so.

"Why did you feel rejected?" Ian prodded gently.

Again Rian was forced to look at a replay of the scene. He studied the actions of the boy, watching his passionate plea for help; how, although he accepted the Hanta's gift, he also ignored it without gratitude; how he also ignored the beautiful flow of love with which the Ancient One greeted him. He seemed to be blind to what was being given him or, in the absence of blindness, he was dissatisfied, asking for something that he didn't need. In every sense, the boy had rejected the Ancient One.

Rian was struck by the realization.

"And now, at last, you know," Ian said. "All this time you have been suffering from your own feelings."

The great camouflage was suddenly removed from all of Rian's life. He saw his insatiable hunger for love as his inability to love, and he understood why he had been such an easy prey for the negative powers of the Pink Prince. In the negative worlds love was not the detached, universal love of the Ancient One, but rather it was the emotional and the possessive hold placed on another. It was why he had felt trapped into the Prince's service and had felt that there was no way out.

Then Rian remembered how Deetra had helped free him from the Pink Prince. She had tricked him into joining her in a search for Curtser and then, at the right moment, certainly Rian's most vulnerable moment, she returned to him the crystal Hanta had given to him. In that moment Rian had realized the love that the Ancient One had bestowed upon him by giving him the crystal. And now Rian knew too that the Ancient One had never rejected him, but that he had rejected the Ancient One.

Ian was smiling gently in a way that said he understood. "You are not the only one to have experienced such a test," he said.

"A test?" Rian asked, looking deeply into Ian's keen eyes. "In what way was it a test?"

"It was a test you demanded for yourself," Ian said. "In seeking the Hanta's love, you rejected it so that you could experience the various levels of emotions, readying yourself to accept Divine, universal love. You chose the experience that led you to this point."

Rian was too astonished to speak. He thought of the awful turmoil he had encountered on Moonwalk, his captivity with the Pink Prince, and all the fear and loneliness he had suffered along the way. Were these things he experienced truly by choice?

"Yes," Ian answered. "Each of us has a life and fills it with experiences of our own choosing. It often takes a great many lifetimes to become aware of this point."

The great void surrounding Ian reminded Rian that he was in the presence of the Great One. He had been drawn into the circle of Hanta consciousness because.... A slow uneven realization crept closer to him. He was in the circle of Hanta consciousness now because he had chosen the experience.

Rian looked to Ian, the Hanta.

In the light about the Hanta he saw every adventure in his life, every experience, every circumstance as a personal choice. He had been born an orphan to be reared by the Elders to prepare him for his life work as scribe and to prepare him for this moment of realization within the Hanta

[58]

consciousness.

"And where do you wish to go from here?" Ian asked.

Rian knew that the Hanta had heard the understanding of his heart. "I don't know," he said. "Being your scribe is all I know."

"Then let the work lead you," Ian said.

Rian remembered the scroll he had given to Deetra. The memory disturbed him. He could feel the vibration of it prickle through his veins. Then he caught control of himself and looked into the Hanta's loving eyes.

"What do you wish of me?" Rian asked.

"What is it you wish for yourself?"

"To serve the Divine Force."

"Then BE as you wish to be. Function in the most natural way. When you feel yourself relaxed and comfortable both within and without, then you will know you are serving the Divine Force." The words trailed off into the silence, resounding as though an echo. "JUST BE!" the Divine One said again and, as the words were spoken, the image of Ian began to fade; the light of Hanta was dimmed and gone.

Vanished!

Rian stood immobile as if he expected the light to reappear. He turned about and studied the empty hall. What was he to do now? The Hanta had said for him to be himself; to be relaxed and comfortable about himself. He thought he knew what the Hanta meant. He would return to his chambers to solve the mysteries set before him as a scribe.

Rian paced his chamber floor absently, then caught himself. There was no reason to be impatient. Ian had not asked him to retreat or to wait. He had said merely that Rian was to go and be himself, living as he felt he wanted to live. It had been Rian's choice to return to his chambers and wait and he felt foolish for it, yet the feeling of expectancy seemed to command him there.

He tried to relax. The timing for his next step should be easy and perfect if he could only relax and allow himself the freedom of going with the natural flow of things. He must let go of the tension and function within the moment. Yet something within would not relax so he sat down at his work table.

The scriptures had taught him much about the power flow that superimposed and controlled all of life. It was a precision time watch and once set in motion perfectly monitored the continuity of a day. He reached for the scroll that explained the power flow and opened it. He read:

> *The power flow is otherwise termed the creative force and it flows from and between and within all beings and things, both animate and inanimate. It supercedes communication between minds and ignites communication between consciousnesses'. It provides the intermediate link with Soul and communicates its bonds.*

Rian loosened his grip on the parchment and permitted the scroll to roll closed in his hand. Then he put it back on the shelf, questioning the expectancy he felt, remembering a time when he had been a boy growing up in Sarpent's household. The Chief Elder had told him not to rush about his tasks anxious for the next moment, that in rushing he would have to wait at the point of completion, but he had not understood and had rushed anyway. When he had finished his tasks he sat anxiously waiting for the Elder's return, wondering at Sarpent's words: "Every task has an allotted time. Too slow or too fast is out of the rhythm of the natural order of things. You must learn to move, pacing yourself with the flow."

What did that have to do with now?

He was not rushing.

He was feeling expectancy.

It was not the same thing.

Or was it?

He leaned back in his chair. He did not have to wait. He could relax completely and go to sleep. He closed his eyes, but at the same time there was a light knock on his chamber door. He jumped to his feet, hurried to the door and opened it. Deetra was on the other side.

"Come in," Rian said, stepping back out of the way for her to enter.

"I am leaving for awhile," she said, taking Rian by the hand. "Sarpent has been asked to journey to the East and to set Hanta's affairs in order there. I will be going with him." She smiled at his surprise. "I was hoping you'd teach my class in spiritual law during my absence," she said. "I would be very grateful."

"You are travelling with Sarpent?"

"Yes." She chuckled at the expression on her friend's face, recalling how in previous times they had used the Chief Elder's name in awe, somewhat frightened by him.

There was a long pause.

"Then he knows about Ian?" Rian asked.

"He may know, but perhaps he is not aware that he knows," Deetra said.

Rian moved restlessly from foot to foot. How could he know and not be aware that he knew? Was the Chief Elder being dishonest with himself? As a parent the Elder was strict beyond words. He had insisted on honesty from Rian in the sharpest sense.

"None of us is immune from the trickery of mind," Deetra reminded. "We can only be as honest as our awareness permits, and sometimes when awareness comes we reject it." She hesitated, studying Rian. "Why do we do it?"

"Because we're in spiritual shock," Rian answered, raising his eyes, as if remembering something.

"Yes, go on," she said, encouraging him.

"The scriptures," Rian said, "relate that spiritual shock is a traumatic realization that follows an emotional combustion."

"How interesting."

"Yes," he said thoughtfully. "I had never really thought about it before." Silently he wondered if Ian had called the Elder to his chamber as he had done him; if he had met Sarpent in the light and sound of the void and Sarpent had rejected him.

"The transformation of the Hanta consciousness from one human form to another is often a difficult and delicate transition for some to accept," Deetra said. "And those closest to the source are sometimes blinded by it."

Rian was quiet and thoughtful. His concern was not for Sarpent but about how one so dedicated to the Hanta could also deny him.

"It is not wise to pass judgment on another," she said. "A judgment can demand that we experience for ourselves that which we have judged."

Deetra knew his thoughts. She also understood what he was feeling.

"When do you leave?" Rian asked, changing his focus of attention.

"Day after tomorrow."

"So soon?"

She nodded.

"Is Ian staying here?"

"For now," she said, uncertain.

"Just the two of you are going?"

Deetra chuckled at his expression. "Just the two of us," she said.

Rian shook his head, disbelieving.

"Unless you'd like to join us," she said, teasing.

Rian lowered his eyes. It was not what he'd like to do. He did not wish to travel anywhere with Sarpent, or to go anywhere near Lord Casmir or Curtser. He did not wish to make the journey to the East. He wished to continue on with his work as scribe. "No," he said finally, "but I will work with your spiritual law class."

"Good." She smiled, knowing that her class was in good hands. "That will put my mind at ease, and it will give you a chance to see Tolar again."

"Have you seen him?"

"No, but then we haven't had class. I expect he will be there."

Rian recalled how Tolar had panicked and run from the sanctuary. He seemed to be suffering from delusions as much as from illusions.

"I'm sure you will find a way to help Tolar," she said.

Rian looked at her, unsure, then he changed the subject. "Do you expect to see Curtser?" he asked.

"I would like to."

"Will you tell him of Ian?"

"Only that he is my husband. The rest is not for me to tell."

Rian would have liked to ask why, but didn't. He knew better and he also knew that Curtser would discover the transition of the Hanta consciousness in his time, as would Sarpent.

Deetra looked to the stack of scrolls on Rian's table. "And you, I see, have much work to do here."

"Much!"

There was a long pause between them, and yet it was a timeless pause in which Rian focused all of his attention on the *Mark,* the scroll that puzzled him. Then he thought of the *Happiness Song* and how its theme was the mark. "How long ago do you suppose the *Happiness Song* was written?" he asked.

"My father remembers it from his childhood and his father before that," Deetra said.

"Had you ever heard of the mark?" Rian asked.

"No, at least it was never discussed."

"Had your father?"

"Perhaps in the same way, knowing but not being aware that he knew," she suggested. "I had never thought about the song before I read the scroll that you gave to Ian and myself."

Rian appeared interested. "Had Ian heard of the mark?"

"Perhaps you should ask him yourself," Deetra said.

Rian looked deeply into his friend's face but he could not tell if she had discussed the matter with Ian.

"I'm sure you'll find your answers," she said after a while.

Rian was annoyed. What did she mean "your answers"? Were not his answers the answers? He was the scribe of the Silent One, working for the All. His job was of importance to many, or was it?

Rian looked away unsure. The pale late afternoon sunlight entered the window, forming a delicate pattern on the ledge. Light and shadow—they seemed to be everpresent, balancing the forces of nature. It was a state of being, the balanced state, the middle path.

What was he thinking?

What reference point did his thoughts have to do with his work as scribe?

Somehow his mind had slipped from the subject of his annoyance—or so it seemed. Then he remembered his meeting with Ian; how he had learned that all experiences were set up by personal choice. It was his attitude toward them that determined the condition of balance or lack of it between light and shadow. His position as scribe was natural to him. Its importance related to himself. Others were only indirectly affected by it.

Why then had he been annoyed at Deetra's statement?

The answer crept toward him like a suspecting foe. It was the same reason he had believed the Ancient One's rejection of him when he first received the crystal; and now it offended him when Deetra placed the matter of the altered scroll's importance on him. Doubtless he would find it in other areas as well, lurking in moments past and waiting in moments to come.

[*64*]

Rian had become aware of his ego.

He turned toward Deetra and looked sadly into his friend's face. He knew she had heard his thoughts. There were no secrets among the Askan. They reflected each other's inner images like polished stones.

Deetra reached for Rian's hand and squeezed it. "Don't worry," she said softly. "I too am just learning."

Rian flushed appreciatively. "A few moments ago I was passing judgment on Sarpent and now I have judged myself."

Deetra laughed. "That's the way it works," she said.

CHAPTER 5

Hanta walked beneath the stone arch just outside of the village gathering place.

He was the Ancient One.

Sarpent was quick on his heels, silently explaining in some detail the preparations for the journey. He felt tense, unheard, foreign in the presence of the master and it disturbed him.

Something was different.

The countenance of the Ancient One seemed to conceal the facsimile of a younger man, as if another being was emerging through the flesh of the Hanta. The effect was unsettling to Sarpent, yet he related the necessary facts with the poise expected of him.

The time of departure had been set with Deetra for the following day. She was alerted to prepare for an indefinite length of time. He had not told her, however, that the purpose of the journey was to pave the way for the transfiguration of the great consciousness.

The communication stopped.

A sudden disturbance gripped Sarpent. It rushed through him. He knew he could conceal nothing from the Ancient One and so he didn't try. It was that same fearful feeling he had experienced following Awakening Day, aware that the master was soon to translate, and anxious about whose form the Hanta consciousness was to assume.

It would enter into one and reside there for perhaps a lifetime. Was the journey to the East to notify this person?

The Ancient One stopped and turned to Sarpent, then he leaned forward and kissed him gently on the cheek.

Sarpent was stunned by the gesture, flushed by the warmth of it, knowing instantly that the Ancient One had heard the churning of his mind with compassion. He must question no more. He must act with obedience and inner silence, and whatever the Great One wished him to know would be forthcoming. Then he became aware of the magnificent music of the spheres. Gazing into the Hanta's eyes, it seemed to lure him, calling him to follow and, as he relaxed and moved with it, he heard a part of himself calling out:

"The Mark! The Mark!"

What did it mean?

The response seemed long in coming and, when it did it came in images, one overlapping the other, both infusing and defusing and Sarpent knew that these were the circumstances of material life as viewed through the spiritual. He could see but even his keen spiritual eyes could not focus sharply enough to capture the meaning of what he saw. It was this realization that told him one thing for certain. He was not the chosen one for the Hanta consciousness.

The realization seemed to empower him, release him, and nourish him. He no longer cared which form the consciousness chose. He would serve as the Elder closest to the master and serve with joy at the responsibility. He was now at peace with himself and filled with the freedom of his release.

The Hanta leaned forward and kissed him lightly again, this time on the other cheek, and it was as though a rainbow spread out before him, igniting a blast of brilliant white light. As the intensity faded, there were again images, only now the images were quite plain. He saw Ian's face and the

[67]

face of Deetra, his wife, at the time of their marriage. He also saw something else, something he had seen in their union during the ceremony but could not quite grasp. It was an overlapping, a dual beingness, something that he could not yet touch upon.

IT WILL COME came the reply from within.

Sarpent released the image and, as the light faded even more, he saw that the Ancient One had gone.

He was alone in the gathering place.

Deetra awoke as a shaft of sunlight rested on her face. She looked about for Ian and saw him sitting on a large rock a few feet away from the tree where she rested. The clear, green, open field stretched out far beyond him. At the edge of the field was the forest and above it the mountains.

Memories of climbing the towering mountains on journey to Moonwalk with Ian as guide came to her. It had been a difficult climb, yes, but not as difficult as braving the forest alone to encounter the powers of the Pink Prince. Yet it was there that she had met the Dales, those wonderful, invisible creatures of the wood, had discovered her own strengths and weaknesses, and had been reunited with her companions Rian and Curtser. Their adventures had been many and together they had learned and had taken the steps to return for Awakening Day ceremonies. Now the negative force had little power over her or so it seemed.

She rose to her feet and went over to Ian, sitting next to him.

He silently took her hand, lifted it to his lips and kissed it. "I shall miss you greatly," he said softly.

She turned to meet his loving gaze. This was Ian the man, her husband. He was saddened by her forthcoming departure, struck by the loneliness of a parting lover; yet it was he, Ian, the Hanta who had asked her to participate in the journey.

"I shall miss you too," she said, then she turned and looked out onto the lonely field. A rabbit jumped through the tall grass and the movement was comical. "Look!" she said, pointing.

Ian looked. The rabbit's long ears shot up and down as it hopped its way through the field. It would disappear and then reappear again in the tall grass. It was headed toward the edge of the woods.

"He's a messenger for the Dales," Ian said, laughing.

Deetra was struck by the idea.

"I was just joking."

"But perhaps he is," Deetra said.

"Perhaps," Ian said, thoughtfully.

Deetra knew that if they had wanted to know they could have easily known, but then it didn't concern them. The rabbit didn't come to them or near them. There was no indication that it was necessary for them to find out. The scene was merely for their amusement.

There seemed nothing for them to say to one another. The love flow between them was obvious. As far as the journey was concerned, Deetra knew that it was a journey for her to learn, to awaken and realize the enormous responsibility of her identity as wife to the man who served as Hanta. And she would also play a supporting role to those key figures who had not yet realized the transfiguration of the Hanta consciousness. She also knew that in her absence the power would be fulfilling itself, and that she had nothing to concern herself with. They were always protected.

Ian turned to her sweetly after listening to her thoughts. "Beloved, you need only gently nudge me in your thoughts and I will be there."

She smiled warmly at him. "I know," she said, but she also knew that she had to stand alone.

The silence grew long and stark, and in it there were rises, not thoughts or images but highs and lows of feeling between them. At moments, Deetra felt she might weep and

[*69*]

at others she felt the urge to call out in jubilation. It was a peculiar sensation and she knew that Ian was experiencing it as well.

"Time will go by quickly," he said, "and even if it does not, our union is above time and space. We will never really leave each other."

Deetra knew that what Ian said was true. It was the way of the Askan, and as marriage partners their union was even stronger. They would not only share an invisible presence but a visible one as well.

The time had come and Sarpent efficiently readied final preparations for the journey. There were two manservants to help carry the necessary supplies and both Sarpent and Deetra were to strap small knapsacks to their backs as well. They were not as large as the manservants' but then Sarpent was no longer a young man and Deetra was a woman.

Ian was there to see them off. He embraced Deetra for a long moment. Sarpent acknowledged his presence with a nod and, as though ill-at-ease, turned and busied himself with the servants. He called out to Deetra that it was time. Ian released his beloved and good-naturedly waved good-bye.

The journey began.

To Deetra's surprise they headed straight for the forest. They cut through the field in almost exactly the same path that she and Ian had seen the rabbit follow. She remembered how they had laughed at it bobbing up and down in the tall grass, how she wondered if it was acting under instructions from the Dales, and how now she was headed that way, following Sarpent's footsteps. A peculiar sensation raced through her. It was as if she suddenly saw herself as a puppet, her motions enacted by some invisible force. But that was impossible.

Or was it?

Sarpent slowed in the lead and looked back, glancing first at Deetra, and then motioned to the servants to hurry their steps behind her. He offered no explanation in word or thought as to the course their journey would take. They were going East of course, but East was a vast expanse and there were any number of trails they could have chosen.

Deetra stilled her mind and allowed her consciousness to sweep the terrain blankly. She sought impressions from Sarpent, or from the creatures of the field but there were none. Not even the servants, both Askan, broke the inner silence, and so she turned her attention elsewhere. She turned her attention to Ian, chatting with him lightly in thought, telling him of where their journey was first leading them and how they were following the rabbit's trail. Then she remembered the thoughtful look on Ian's face when Deetra had turned their joke of the Dale's messengers into a possible truth. She wondered if Ian had known then, or if her suggestion prompted a reality.

Sarpent slowed and turned to Deetra. In thought he said, "Walk silently, my daughter. Your mind disturbs the flow of movement."

Instantly, Deetra was silent.

They were on the edge of the woods.

Silently, they entered.

The thick forest rose up about them. Deetra scanned the tops of the trees. There was definitely more light coming through than there had been on her previous visit. She was glad, knowing that the Dales' food was light. It was their subsistence and with it they could easily carry out their duties as guardians of the forest and forest creatures.

Looking about as she kept in step with Sarpent, she admired the character of the forest. It had a sparkle to it and wildflowers grew at the bases of trees everywhere.

Sarpent drew the little party to a halt, extending a hand for silence. To Deetra, he asked, "Would you like to call them?"

Deetra's heart jumped a beat. She had not seen or communicated with the Dales for what seemed a very long time. "Yes," she answered, gratefully, "I would."

In her heart, as well as aloud, she called, "Little Dales, are you there? It is Deetra, visiting the forest in the name of the Hanta!"

She waited.

Gradually, a low humming sound rose and then swift movement. It danced about her excitedly, shadow-like forms that could only be seen by swift movement of the eye. The humming turned into voices calling out, "Deetra ... Deetra ... where have you been? Where have you been?"

"I've married Ian," she said, calling back to them.

The little Dales danced faster and faster about her. There was no doubt of their enthusiasm. "She's married to Ian .... She's married to Ian," they called in unison.

Sarpent grew impatient and nudged her, indicating that he wished to speak.

"I am here as special envoy to the East with Sarpent the Chief Elder," she said. "The Hanta has sent us."

The Dales grew suddenly very still. The leader, a shadow of a little man with pointed ears, stepped forward. Deetra was glad to see him.

"Something is different .... Something is different!" chimed the little man with pointed ears. "The Holy One's name brings news of another." Then he fell silent.

"How do you know that?" Sarpent asked uneasily.

"I know ... I know," the little man with pointed ears said. "I can see him .... I can see him!"

Deetra could see the image of Ian in the Dale leader's thought. Surely Sarpent would see it as well.

"There are some things you cannot possibly know about," Sarpent said with authority, but you will, we all will in time."

"But I see ... I see ... and I know ... I know," the

leader said.

The Dales knew!

The Dales recognized Ian as Hanta!

"Be still!" Sarpent commanded.

Deetra was astounded. Sarpent still did not know. He refused to know the Hanta. Looking back to the manservants, she could see that they had been listening and were struck by the news of what the Dales had seen.

"We are here to seek the portal to the East," Sarpent said. "Please lead us there."

"The portal to the East ... the portal to the East!" the Dales called in unison.

"Why do you wish to go there?" the Dale leader asked.

"We bear messages for the Eastern tribes," Sarpent said, "and since we are here in service to the Hanta it is your duty to guide us to the portal."

There was a stir among the Dales and they ran back and forth wildly at the demand. "You don't understand," the little man with pointed ears said, "once you enter through the portal we cannot let you return."

"Nonsense!" Sarpent said, seemingly annoyed.

"No nonsense ... no nonsense," the Dales said in unison. "It's the law of the forest," the leader said. "Once you pass through the portal, you cannot return into the forest again."

"You mean that way, but there are other ways to return," Sarpent said.

"No. No," the leader said. "No return except for the Pink Prince."

The Dales grew deathly still.

Deetra should not have been shocked but she was. Lord Casmir was the only Eastern tribesman to visit their village and she knew now who he was. Was that why Curtser had not returned, or visited? He could not do so!

"That is not so," Sarpent said. "And now you will do as requested and lead us to the portal."

Sarpent did not know about Lord Casmir.

Or did he?

Ian would not send his wife to the land of the East if it were true that there could be no return.

Or would he?

Ian was Hanta!

Deetra could feel that her thoughts had been heard by the Dales. They were clustered tightly, protectively about her. She wished she could spend more time with them now, to comfort them and herself, yet if Hanta wanted her to go to the East with Sarpent she would go.

At her decision, the Dales backed off. "Will you take us?" she asked them.

"We will do as you ask .... We will do as you ask," they answered softly in unison.

"Then let us be on our way," Sarpent said.

The portal was a round, dark hole through the mountain. They stood before the entrance of it, Sarpent in the lead behind the Dales. He turned to look at his little party. "Are you ready?" he asked, looking from face to face.

There was no doubt in Deetra's mind that she was to go, or that Sarpent was to go, but the land to the East was unknown and their return uncertain. It did not seem necessary that the manservants accompany them.

"Did Hanta request you to take these men to the East?" Deetra asked Sarpent.

Sarpent glared at the girl. It was not usual for his authority to be questioned. Still, she had a point. If the outcome was uncertain as the Dales indicated, there was no use involving unnecessary persons.

He looked to the manservants. "You will carry your packs to the far end of the tunnel and leave them there. Then you are to return to our village and report what has happened." Sarpent paused, looking deeply into each man's face. "Never fear," he said confidently, "we will return."

The Dales drew close about Deetra. Their warmth and concern for her safety deeply touched her. She knew she was loved.

"I will be all right," she said, petting the shadows clutching about her legs, "and I will return."

The Dale leader tugged at her hand.

She bent down to him.

"The secret," he said. "Remember the secret." The other Dales mimicked his words, "The secret . . . . The secret," they said in sing-songy voice.

"No, what is it?" Deetra asked, sensing that Sarpent was growing impatient.

"Remember the secret that you once rediscovered for us," the little man with pointed ears said. "We are pure energy and that is how we balance the negative and positive forces for survival in the material worlds."

"Yes, I do remember that," Deetra said, "but you cannot go with us to the East."

"Not our form but the energy can," the leader said. "We have learned much since you last met with us. We have learned how to assist man."

"How?"

"As neutral energy."

"But how can we use you?"

"Call our names," the Dale said, "but call it in a special way. Call it: Daa-lless in a drawn out way. It will summon the energy force that is waiting to be called by ITS name."

"That rise you feel," the leader explained, "is the balance of the forces. When you call it, it happens. Got it?"

"Yes, thank you Dales," she said appreciatively.

"You helped us. Now we help you!" the Dales called out in unison.

Sarpent had been listening curiously. He didn't know what to expect on the other side of the mountain, but he was a man wise enough to tune in to the relation of power sources when offered. He bowed appreciatively and then politely remarked that it was time they were on their way.

They entered the portal and were instantly enveloped by darkness. Sarpent moved slowly but with confidence and Deetra and the other Askan moved easily behind him. It was not Sarpent who led them but the audible life stream, the sound current, the beautiful haunting sounds of the inner worlds. As Askan there was never any discomnfort in darkness. The sound was always with them.

They reached the end of the tunnel. They knew they had come to it by the thin streak of light that waited a few feet ahead. Sarpent turned to the manservants. He thanked them for their assistance and told them to leave their bundles and to return to the village.

Obediently, the men did as they were told, turned, and went back through the mountain.

CHAPTER 6

Sarpent and Deetra stepped into a world that seemingly had two suns. There was the sun overhead and an equally dazzling ball of fire reflected in the lake spread out in front of them. Both seemed responsible for the luminous effect of this world and Deetra was surprised that the East should be so different from where they came from in the West.

Sarpent seemed equally surprised. In thought he recalled memories of stories he had heard of the wonderful East; of its magnificent color and light and the excellence of its inhabitants' lives. He had heard many of these stories from Casmir. Before he had felt them to be exaggeration and now he wasn't sure. Why wasn't he sure? He could see for himself the beauty of what had been described to him, yet something within cautioned and it cautioned firmly. He turned to Deetra. "What do you see, my daughter?" he asked. The question was asked in the familiar tone of the Chief Elder.

Looking about, Deetra chose her answer carefully. She had heard the thoughts of the Chief Elder and his recollections of what the Lord Casmir had told him and she also knew Casmir's true identity. "My senses tell me that I see one thing, and Soul tells me I see another," she said finally.

Sarpent studied the young woman next to him. There was no doubt that she had acquired wisdom, one of the great aspects of mastership. It pleased him to have one of the flock be so atuned. "What do your senses tell you?" Sarpent asked.

Deetra withdrew from Sarpent's gaze and again looked out over the landscape. "I see land and I see water and I see the spectacular event of two suns illuminating a colorful scene of undefined nature." She looked to Sarpent.

"And what does Soul tell you?" Sarpent asked.

"Soul tells me that my senses are being deceived," she said.

"I quite agree," Sarpent said. "Is there anything more?"

"No," she said, unsure.

"I'm sure our perceptions will deepen as we continue our journey," the Elder said, motioning for her to follow him. The rest of their supplies would remain and later be retrieved.

There was a deep silence to the air. Although everywhere was the appearance of nature and natural things, there was no sound coming forth—no birds, no small animals, no insects, and no wind to disturb the vague impressions of trees and shrubs. The countryside seemed unreal, as it would disappear if touched. Even the effect of the burning suns seemed to be just a colorful display, a mockup of some kind. As they moved through it, Deetra following Sarpent, she had a flash of the feeling she encountered when first she, Rian, and Curtser had set foot on Moonwalk on their way to Awakening Day.

They had gone quite a distance when Sarpent turned back to Deetra. She could see by his expression that he had been experiencing similar awarenesses. "It seems we are in some sort of entranceway," he said thoughtfully.
"Would you agree?"

"Yes," she said, nodding as she answered. She caught a glimpse of someone and something moving about in the distance. "And I believe we are nearly out of it." She pointed and Sarpent turned around to see what had caught her attention.

There was nothing there.

Sarpent waited, looking in the direction Deetra had indicated. He had reason to trust her senses.

Suddenly, a form darted in and out of the landscape. It was followed by something.

Sarpent motioned Deetra to follow and the two of them hurried on their way toward what they had seen. It should not have taken them more than a few minutes.

But it did.

They walked and walked some more. The distance was indefinable. It seemed to go on and on like illusion, not really taking them anywhere, not really coming from anywhere. Finally they stopped.

Sarpent drew his great form erect and looked out over the terrain. There was nothing but an infinity of what they had travelled through. "My little sister," he said affectionately, "we seem to be the object of trickery. It is evident that someone is out there spelling illusion about us, luring us, however we will go no further until our host makes himself known."

Deetra was aware that the Chief Elder had addressed her as little sister and it pleased her. It also pleased her that he had taken a stand in their behalf. Although she was not in the least fatigued, she too had the distinct feeling that some force was trying to occupy them with motion. She moved next to Sarpent and stood looking into the terrain with him.

They waited.

Then it became apparent that the force that had lured them was now yielding to their demands. It happened very gradually. At first there was a sigh that filled the air and then the sigh began to materialize. Directly in front of them a mountain took form and the size of it was tremendous, towering up and beyond their line of vision, becoming lost in a milk-white cloud. The mountain was definitely solid but it was also translucent, with orange hues pulsating from it.

"And now we see!" Sarpent said triumphantly.

Deetra was too astounded to speak. She was glad to be with Sarpent whose wits she felt were more predictable.

The great mountain rolled a beam of irridescent orange light toward them, stopping only inches in front of their feet. The beam seemed to indicate a path for them to follow.

Deetra took a step backward.

Sarpent turned to her. "What does Soul tell you now, little sister?" he asked.

She hesitated, shifting her attention to Sarpent. "It tells me that we are being confronted by a powerful force."

He nodded in agreement. "Would you propose that we ignore it and find another way to the villages?" he asked.

She raised herself to her full erect height and looked deeply into the orange hue that made a path in front of them. It seemed to come even more alive under her gaze, as though an entity held it firmly at their feet. She allowed herself to feel its strength without yielding to it and, while doing so, she also felt something else. The sensation was unexpected and so it was difficult to define and grasp at first, but gradually she grew to accept the feeling from it as friendly.

She turned to Sarpent who had recognized the identification. "I feel it is all right for us to go with it," she said.

"Then let us go," Sarpent said.

Stepping onto the path, Deetra saw that they sank up up to their knees into the orange hue; that it was more than light; that it was part of the entity of the mountain and that it had intelligence. Moving through it was a form of communication. It spoke in impressions and images and they were able to answer in like manner.

"Why is it you seek the mountain of light?" it asked.

They replied that they didn't seek the mountain of light, that they were there on a special mission from Hanta, the Ancient One, and that they were returning a visit from

Lord Casmir, wishing also to see Curtser and to walk among the communities of the East.

The mountain of light seemed to acknowledge their mission. Its light grew more brilliant, intensifying the orange hue and, as the glow expanded within it, Deetra and Sarpent were moved hurriedly along its path.

Deetra felt as though she was being sucked into the mountain. She clung to the back of Sarpent's robe, noticing that the Elder had his mind under perfect control and that he had no thoughts at all about what was happening to them; consequently, he moved easily and without hurry.

The light drew them beneath the flesh of the mountain, into the heart of it. Within, the light was more manageable. There was order and form. It illuminated a long narrow hallway and on either side the walls were covered with great murals, scenes of another civilization.

"What you see is the history of the East," the mountain pulsed. "It was once the highest of civilizations. Its records were filled with heroes and spiritual giants. It was here that the first Hanta consciousness was formed and it is here that all else will end."

What did it mean?

Deetra was cautioned to steady her thoughts by an impulse from Sarpent. She continued to study the hallway murals, astounded by inventions of matter-vehicles, which were used to transport large numbers of people through the air, as though the people were sitting inside a huge bird and flying from one place to another. And there were devices that could explode and destroy whole cities, and other war weapons of peculiar strength. It seemed to be an unlikely home of spiritual giants, but perhaps . . . .

Sarpent raised a hand to silence her.

Thought had once again dominated her.

How could she stop it?

Telepathically, Sarpent indicated that she should place her attention on the third eye and leave it there, that there would be plenty of time for thinking on these things later. Then he motioned her to continue following him down the long corridor. He did not look either way, using his peripheral vision to view the murals as they passed.

Seeing them in this way, the murals became animated with life. Huge structures were built by people operating machines and the machines, in turn, had a way of operating the people. It was impossible to tell which was manipulating which and the effects of the building and destroying inter-relationships seemed to cause a breakdown in the physical appearance of the life that lived there, in the society. The people were mental beings and the machine-beings that they created became greater mental beings than those who created them. Human-kind seemed to bow down to its creation and, as it did, the machine grew in power and dominated the land. Eventually, the murals showed that the world was destroyed by this machine-power. What of the spiritual giants the mountain referred to?

Deetra quickly silenced the thought. At the end of the hallway was a globe of orange light. It was like a barrier of some sort, a doorway into another world. They started through it. Bells sounded, ringing all about them. The ringing was harsh at first, loud and deafening, then gradually the bells softened, becoming a soft tinkling sound. Then they stopped.

Ahead of them, dressed in orange robes, was Curtser. He appeared like a god, a reigning entity who lived within the mountain. Sarpent remembered him as her travelling companion to Moonwalk, as the one without a crystal who had acquired the pink jewel of creation. He was a brave, determined young man who dared combat with the Pink Prince, but who also had enslaved himself to the Prince's power by desiring to overpower him. Still, looking at her friend, Deetra could not hide her joy. She hurried forward and kissed him lightly on the cheek.

Curtser stepped back, withdrawing from her.

Deetra studied his expressionless face. He had aged considerably but the familiar expression of his sensitive eyes was still apparent. He returned her affection in glance. Then she saw that there were others behind him, maybe four or five hidden by the orange mist. They seemed to be looking at him, waiting, as if he was their leader.

"It is good to see you," she said aloud to Curtser.

"What brings you here?" he asked.

Sarpent stepped forward. "We are here in service to the Ancient One," he said.

"In what way?" Curtser asked, turning to face Sarpent. The softness in his eyes disappeared.

"Perhaps I should first speak to the Lord Casmir," Sarpent said. He stood firmly in front of the younger man.

"Lord Casmir is without position here," Curtser said. "If you wish to pass through this land it is with my permission."

There was a long moment of silence in which both men looked deeply into one another.

"Where are we?" Deetra asked, purposely interrupting.

Curtser yielded in his gaze upon Sarpent and turned to her. There was a long moment in which he did not answer and his mental imagery was unclear, as though he did not know. "I'm not entirely sure where," he said finally. "We happened on the mountain as you did and we remained. It is a sort of limbo place but powerful, exceedingly powerful."

Deetra recalled the feeling of power coming from the mountain before they had entered and she knew what he said was true. "How long have you been here?" she asked.

"We escaped and found our way here a short time ago," Curtser said.

"Escaped from what?" Sarpent asked.

"Did you not notice the unreal appearance of form before entering the mountain?"

"Of course," Deetra said, remembering the feeling of

the land, as if she and Sarpent had been lured into an illusion-ary world. "It reminded me somewhat of Moonwalk, which was ruled by the Pink Prince."

"Yes," Curtser said, nodding. "Only here the Pink Prince is known as the Lord Casmir."

"How absurd!" Sarpent said.

"Is it!" Curtser said, raising his hand. "It is the truth." Between his fingers was the pink jewel of creation and, as he held it, it seemed to expand in size and become alive with images. "See into the Akashic record for yourself," Curtser said. "Herein are the true identities of all life."

Sarpent stood motionless, watching the overlapping images of the Pink Prince and Lord Casmir. They flowed one into the other and he saw how the disguise distinguished the negative force as a noble leader among the people.

The images stopped and Curtser lowered his hand, tucking the jewel into a compartment beneath his robe. "And so you see," he said.

"It cannot be! Lord Casmir could be next in line to become Hanta," Sarpent said defensively. Then he grew quiet, silently staring into space, remembering his previous feelings toward Casmir, how he had considered him to be the next Hanta, a holy one.

Curtser looked at the Elder in surprise but did not speak.

Deetra lowered her eyes respectfully. She had guessed that Sarpent had not known the identity of Casmir and she knew that this moment of discovery would have to come. She was glad that it came without undue experiences early in their journey; still she felt a deep compassion for the Elder. His thoughts lashed out at the announcement, fight-ing it, and she could not help but see the painful memory of Sarpent considering that Lord Casmir was to be Hanta. He had confused the negative force with the positive and now stood stripped of the confidence of his rank.

Deetra raised her eyes to meet Curtser's. She could not

hide the compassion she felt and it seemed to influence Curtser, to soften his surprise into like feeling.

"What is it you wish of me?" he asked softly. "You are here for another reason than to see that I am well."

Deetra answered telepathically. In her mind's eye she told Curtser of her marriage to Ian and in imagery she related the identity of Ian.

Sarpent was not aware of their communication. He was not aware of anything outside of his own turmoil.

Curtser did not appear surprised but took Deetra's hand warmly and kissed it. "I am very happy for you, my friend," he said.

"You seem to have already known," Deetra said.

"No, not consciously anyway, but I did know that some great inner activity was taking place," Curtser said, thoughtfully.

"In what way?"

"Casmir has been creating havoc everywhere. Usually, the Lord of the negative worlds is more subtle. Now his rampage is holocaust, destructive beyond any memory of him, and his destructiveness has seemed to be filled with urgency and purpose." Curtser paused, turning to Sarpent and then to face Deetra again. "Casmir has left his mark everywhere. He offends the East with upheaval and the West with illusion. He dares to win the confidence of such spiritual Elders as Sarpent."

Curtser had referred to Casmir's mark.

"What of it?" Curtser asked.

Deetra briefly related Rian's work as scribe; how he came upon the scroll about the mark; and how he was disturbed by the presence of a second handwriting, making notations in the margins. "But the notations were not contrary to the rest of the scroll," she said, meaning that they could not have been added by Casmir.

Curtser did not answer, but from his silence Deetra was aware that Casmir's negative influence was often so subtle that it seemed not to be contrary to the positive. It was possible that Casmir was responsible for the notations. She wondered if Rian had thought on the matter.

"The positive force has manifested in a younger body," Curtser said thoughtfully. "It would seem that Casmir has tried to equal its strength in opposite force. The Eastern people have suffered greatly."

"Then why do you stay in the East? Why have you not returned to your own village?"

Curtser looked at Deetra with distant eyes. "I will try to explain," he said. "When you, Rian, and myself arrived at the City of Light, when we received the blessing of the Ancient One on the platform amid the Askan, we individually chose our roles of service to the positive force. Rian chose his role as scribe, you as a channel within the village and later the wife of the Holy One, and myself as a way-shower in another plane of existence." He paused, looking deeply into his friend's eyes. "I can see you are somewhat confused," he said.

"Somewhat," she answered.

"You have noticed that I am not alone," Curtser said.

"Yes."

"Those with me are learning to recognize and dispel illusion. They found me after losing their way."

"Then you are their guide," Deetra said, trying to understand.

"Yes, only in guiding, I am also learning the way," Curtser said.

"Then you are not in opposition with Lord Casmir," Deetra said, somewhat puzzled.

"Not directly," Curtser answered. "I have finally learned that opposition builds and strengthens the resistance. It has taken me a long time to come to this point in my self-control. Although I had known that principle intellectually, I could not until recently practice what I knew."

"But you do not have to stay here," Deetra said. "You

would be welcome in your village and in your home."

"Thank you," Curtser said, smiling, "but I have already chosen my life's service to the Hanta. There are those lost souls who require assistance and I wish to help them find the way."

"Find the way to where?" Deetra asked. "You said before that you did not know where we were or the nature of the mountain."

"I did not say I did not know the nature of the mountain," Curtser said, correcting her.

Deetra studied her friend curiously. "Then what is the nature of the mountain?" she asked. She wasn't meaning to challenge him but she was trying to understand. Something in what Curtser was saying did not make sense to her. Something he had said was not within spiritual law, or so it seemed.

"Its light is orange," Curtser said, motioning with his hand to the color about them.

"Yes."

"Orange is the color of the causal plane," he said.

Deetra was astounded by his answer and did not speak.

"We are on the plane of cause and effect. It is the world of the occult as well as the world where the Akashic Records are kept. Here is the history of all civilization, as well as the history of each individual within it. Surely, you saw the murals within the mountain?"

Deetra nodded, remembering the animated stories of machines and man. She particularly recalled an image of a machine that carried hundreds of people through the air, flying them from one place to another.

"The secret of the causal plane," Curtser said, "is that what *was* IS and what *is* WILL BE. In other words, the past is the present and the present will be the future. Whatever we do will bring a like effect."

"I understand the principle," Deetra said, still unsure of where Curtser was leading her in thought. "But is it that

[87]

you are teaching these principles to those with you?"

"I am helping them understand the spiritual law behind the principle," Curtser said. "But mainly I encourage them to be conscious of their right to choose and to choose every step for themselves. We are born with this freedom to live as CAUSE and to be our own effect."

Deetra was beginning to see why Ian had requested her to join Sarpent on this journey. Not only was she to be a helpmate to him but to those working on other planes of existence. Ian had not discussed Curtser but surely he had known that Deetra would learn of her friend's activities and broaden in understanding. She and Sarpent had entered through the portal of the East. The land had reminded her of Moonwalk as indeed it should. They had entered the inbetween worlds. That was why the Dales had shown such concern, uncertain that they would be able to return, and offered the strength of their energy to help draw them back when necessary.

Deetra related her recent meeting with the Dales to Curtser.

Curtser nodded appreciatively. Although his memories of the Dales were mostly in times of stress, he felt a gentle fascination for them and he knew of their concern regarding the safety of the forest, how they exercised neutral energy, thus working always to keep the balance. Then he said, "But they cannot manifest here."

"I suppose not, but they did say I could call on them in an emergency," Deetra said. "They told me of a certain way to call them."

Curtser looked at her doubtfully, and then turned the subject back to his mission. "We are trying to reach the land of Sohang," he said. "We will stay here only as long as necessary."

"And where is Sohang?" Deetra asked, unsure of what Curtser meant. Sohang she had heard was an invisible place.

"Not so invisible here in the inbetween worlds," Curtser said, answering her thought. "Of course, we will have to make it BE somewhere through our imaginations before it can appear. But that is why we landed here in the causal plane, the memory plane, so that we can discover our way."

Deetra looked deeply into her friend. She wished to respect his mission, but it all seemed so futile, almost to the point of being ridiculous. She was sure that he knew a great deal about illusion—the memory plane and Sohang or mental plane—but what was the point? He could dwell in the pure, positive God-worlds instead.

"Not so!" Curtser said, his fists poised angrily on his hips. He had heard Deetra's thoughts.

Once again Deetra was to suffer the consequences of her thoughts. "I am sorry," she said. "The adventures you choose are none of my affair. I have no right to judge you."

"Indeed you don't," Curtser said, annoyed. "But then my adventures must be somewhat your affair, as well as Sarpent's, or else you wouldn't be here with me."

Deetra was astonished.

She was here because the Hanta sent her here for experience. Sarpent, as well, was here for the experience. They could no more dwell in the pure, positive God-worlds than Curtser. They first needed more experience in the lower worlds. The lower worlds, all of them, were under the influence of the negative force. They had been sent to Lord Casmir because he was the ruler of this force. It was within his domain that they all required experiences.

Deetra argued the point within herself. Could it be that the wife of Hanta was not worthy? Surely there were others who needed this training more than herself. What of Rian? She turned to Sarpent, touching the Chief Elder lightly on the arm. Was Sarpent not above such meager treatment? She had always felt him to be the pillar of the village. His inner strength and his self-control always seemed so impeccable. Gradually she forgot herself and closed her fingers tightly about Sarpent's arm. The gesture seemed to call him out of his trance.

Sarpent looked to Deetra and covered her hand with his. "We will make it, little sister," he said. "There is something that we, individually, need to learn and we will learn it."

Sarpent had recovered from the shock of Lord Casmir's identity.

"You and I," Sarpent said softly, "are discovering that we are still very much touched by pride. Inwardly, we ask how could one of our stature be so fooled when the real question is *what is it that I need to recognize to overcome the fool in me?*" He stepped back and turned to Curtser. "What is your next move?"

Curtser folded his arms across his chest. "There can be no next move until the imagination has prepared itself," he said. "I have chosen to help the others because I have the jewel of creation, a powerful force of the negative power."

"How well I remember," Sarpent said, recalling how the young man had appeared before him at Bell Rock before Awakening Day and how Sarpent had instructed him to learn to use its power. "And now you will have the opportunity to demonstrate what you have learned."

Curtser lowered his eyes. "I have learned not to use the power," he said respectfully. "I keep it only to remind myself of that and to verify the visions of the lower worlds."

"You have become a wise young man," Sarpent said.

Curtser raised his eyes to meet Sarpent's. He recalled how he used to fear the Chief Elder and he marvelled at how very comfortable he now felt in his presence. "Thank you," he said. "It is my goal to serve the Hanta as a channel for the Divine Force."

Sarpent nodded appreciatively. "And what of your friends?" he asked, motioning to the forms barely visible in the orange mist behind Curtser.

Curtser moved to one side, extending a hand for them

to come forward. There were five and on invitation they moved swifly from within the mist, stepping into the open.

Rian, Tolar, and Geta were among them.

Could it be?

Deetra was too astonished to speak.

How did they get here?

Who were the other two—an older man and woman. They were clutching each other by the hand.

Deetra turned to Sarpent who seemed as surprised as she at the sight of Rian. He did not appear to know the others.

"Rian, did you follow us?" Sarpent asked.

"Not intentionally," Rian answered shyly.

"How then do you explain your presence here?" Sarpent asked.

Rian thought of answering that he was not sure and then thought better of it. Instead he kept silent.

Sarpent turned his attention to Curtser. "How do you explain this?" he asked.

"Earlier, I explained to Deetra that it was my mission to act as a way-shower for those who become lost in the inbetween worlds. It must be that Rian became lost." Curtser paused, looking at the younger man. He knew he was the sanctuary scribe and he also knew that Rian had been reared by Sarpent and still somewhat feared him. "But then again," Curtser said thoughtfully, "it may be that Rian is acting as a way-shower for those with him."

Suddenly Deetra remembered that she had given Rian charge of her spiritual law class. Both Tolar and Geta were a part of that class. Somehow they had slipped into the inbetween worlds, but how? Especially Geta? She recalled how the girl had acted in class, remarking with such striking fear at any mention of the Hanta's name. How did she have the nerve to be with them? Geta did not appear to be unnerved.

"We are only partially here," Rian said. He drew in a long breath before continuing. "Our physical bodies are still with the others in the class. We were doing an exercise and that exercise related to the intercommunications of the universal mind."

"The first stop would naturally be the causal plane," Curtser said. "It is the trigger to mind power."

"Well, here we are," Rian said confidently, motioning to the others.

"I have not yet met the Hanta," Tolar said shyly, "but I will."

"For what reason?"

"To become awakened," Tolar said.

Sarpent studied the man, the deep, tired lines around the eyes, and then turned to the girl Geta. "And what is your purpose?" he asked her.

"Oh, not to meet the Hanta," she said quickly. "I wish only to share an experience with others."

"And what is this experience you're sharing?" Sarpent asked.

"This?" Geta shifted from foot to foot, uncomfortably. "This is not an experience. We are in class. What is happening here isn't really happening. It's imagination. We are doing an imagination exercise."

"That's true," Rian said. "We are doing an imagination exercise—soul travelling to another dimension."

Deetra chuckled to herself at the irony of Rian's position. He was merely following the class plan she had laid out for him. Neither one of them had thought of the bond between him and Sarpent, or him and her, or Tolar and Geta and her; but all the same, the law of attraction was in operation. After all, the law operated from the causal plane. It was only natural that if all the forces at work were lined up in a particular way, that they would meet just where thay had met.

"All right, little sister, where do we go from here?"

Sarpent asked.

He had heard her thought.

"It seems," she said, that our ways may separate. Rian, Tolar, and Geta are following a classroom exercise and may choose to discontinue it at any time. But who are these two people?"

"I found them together," Curtser said.

"They were not with us in class," Rian said. "And I do not know them."

Deetra turned to the older couple. They were still clinging together, hands clutched. "Where do you come from?" she asked.

The man shrugged his shoulders, and the woman seeing him do this, shook her head.

"Are you from the Eastern villages or the West?" Deetra asked again.

The man shrugged his shoulders again and the woman shook her head.

"Have they communicated with you at all?" Deetra asked Curtser.

"Only that they are frightened," he said. "Perhaps they are truly lost."

"Perhaps," Sarpent added thoughtfully, "but I don't think so." He moved toward them.

The man and woman stepped back to avoid contact with Sarpent.

He moved closer again. As he did there was a flutter in the atmosphere about them. A strong metallic odor seemed to escape from it.

Skunks were not the only creatures who used odors as a defense, Deetra thought. She became aware of it spiralling outward, reaching past Sarpent to her. She called to him in thought.

"Do not be concerned," Sarpent said, telepathically.

Rian and the others had moved away.

Curtser stood next to Deetra.

[93]

Sarpent began to chant HU. Over and over again he chanted the word. Deetra remembered the sound from when she and Ian had chanted it during their wedding procession and she joined Sarpent. Curtser, Rian, and the others joined in as well.

Suddenly the old man and woman began to fade. Their images shimmered at first, as though resisting and then they completely disappeared.

Deetra stood staring into the empty space. "What nature of entity were they?" she asked Sarpent.

"Remember we are on the causal plane," Sarpent said, turning to Deetra. "It is not unusual for an apparition to slip off the time track and present itself. It happens occasionally on the physical plane, so here it must be a frequent occurrence."

It pleased Deetra that Sarpent knew these things but it also mystified her as to why he was with her if he knew. Then, as if some inner presence cautioned her, she dismissed the thought.

"The others are gone as well," Curtser said.

Rian, Tolar, and Geta had disappeared.

"It was time," Sarpent said. "And now, I think it is also time for us to consider our mission, little sister." He wrapped his arm about Deetra's shoulders.

The warmth of the gesture surprised both Deetra and Curtser.

"You wish to journey on to Sohang. Why?" Sarpent asked Curtser.

Curtser looked away momentarily, as though he were trying to hide something. Then he looked directly at Sarpent. "There is more to my mission than helping lost souls," he said, pausing. "I am trying to find my way through the lower worlds so that I may enter the soul plane."

"But you were with Rian and me at the City of Light," Deetra said.

Curtser shifted his eyes shyly, finally resting on

Deetra. "I was with you and Rian," he said, "but I was not aware of being in the City of Light, only that you and Rain said that was where we were."

How could that be?

"It is interesting how we take others' beingness for granted," Sarpent said, glancing at Deetra and then returning his attention to Curtser. "You have chosen the slow road, my son, yet it is no less valid. Although Deetra and Rian have already attained the City of Light, have awakened in soul body, there is still much they do not know about the lower worlds."

That was why Deetra was here. She realized from Sarpent's words that she needed additional experience.

"That is part of the reason," Sarpent said, listening to her thought, "but there is more to it. The rest will be discovered at the right time."

Deetra wondered if Sarpent knew what lay ahead for her.

He turned to her wonderingly and shook his head. Again he had heard her thought. "And neither do I know what is ahead for me," he said.

"May I travel with you?" Curtser asked.

The Chief Elder nodded. "It seems that for now your way and our way is the same," he said.

"Then are we ready to leave?" Curtser asked.

"I don't think so," Deetra said.

Curtser looked at Deetra doubtfully.

"She's right," Sarpent said. "We will not be ready to leave until each of us fully understands the nature of the causal plane. For one the time spent may be shorter than another. One may be ready to leave before another. It is a privilege that must be earned. Once earned we may come here at will. Then, Curtser, you will truly be a guide for lost souls."

As Deetra listened to Sarpent's words she heard the familiar high-pitched sound of the spheres. It occurred to her that the sound was the sound of HU and that the HU was the voice of the supreme deity. She momentarily withdrew within herself, listening. Faintly, somewhere in the distance she heard Sarpent, sharing his knowledge with Curtser, but they seemed a world apart now. She was within—dazzling specks of light danced about her and the sound of HUuuuu pulsed through her. It moved in waves—the light and the sound, the outward wave and the inward. She felt as though she was riding the current of it, deeper and deeper until....

Ian stood shimmering in radiant body before her.

Deetra reached out to him.

He took her hand and lifted it to his lips. The dazzling light around her suddenly flared up like a flame given fuel and for an instant she was blinded by it. When it subsided, Ian was gone.

Sarpent was telling Curtser that they would rest awhile before exploring the causal plane.

CHAPTER 7

Sarpent paced the hard earthen floor, thinking on how he had misjudged Lord Casmir, how the negative force could appear so like the positive even to one who, like himself, was so evenly trained as a servant for the Divine. The razor's edge seemed to become finer and finer as one progressed upon the path, the line so fine that its appearance was influenced by a slight shift of attitude, any sort of inward change or outward motion. The cause of such deception was so delicate. Obviously, he was here in the causal plane to understand that cause, but how?

The answer formed in him slowly. At first he didn't recognize it but then, as he became more and more aware of Deetra's and Curtser's presence, he knew. He was to teach them the essence and secrets of the causal plane as he had been taught years ago and in the teaching the answer would come.

Deetra, at least, had heard Sarpent's thoughts. She was seated next to Curtser on the cold ground when she looked up at the Elder and said, "Then let us begin."

The Chief Elder stopped walking and looked at Deetra and Curtser. It was obvious he was still drifting somewhere in contemplation. Then he spoke. "First of all, we are not within a mountain," he said, "but within the temple of golden wisdom on the causal plane. There are entities here of great power who will assist us if they choose to do so.

They may or may not become visible to us. It is of no consequence. The first thing to remember is all planes of existence from the lower to the higher and vice versa overlap and that no plane within the lower worlds can exist solely unto itself.

"The next thing you are to know," Sarpent said, seating himself in front of the others, "is that each individual has the power to reform the appearance of these lower worlds via mind. We believed that when the orange glow presented itself on the terrain that it was coming from a mountain; therefore, we naturally find ourselves within a mountain, seated on cold, hard earth." He paused, reflectively shifting his glance from Deetra to Curtser.

"The truth is that here within the wisdom temple the floors are crystal, covered by soft orange cushions, where we may rest and enjoy the light of the environment. It is within this warm atmosphere that we will learn together, bonded by common imagery. The walls of this temple are also crystal and the orange hues seem to pulsate from them. The ceiling is open to the sky and to the planes of existence beyond this plane and yet, all planes exist here."

It was as if they had slipped into a dream. The crystal walls and floor and open ceiling were just as Sarpent had said. Instead of sitting on the cold, hard ground, the three of them sat on plush orange cushions, facing each other in a small circle. Light darted about the crystal room. The sight was illuminating and beautiful.

"Now," the Chief Elder said, "let us begin." He hesitated, calling inwardly upon the Lord of the temple to guide his words and to open him as a channel for the Divine Force. "We know that the causal plane is the plane of pure memory, pure in that what is recorded here in the Akashic Record is the truth and reality of what actually IS. It is without interpretation of a recorder. *It simply is as it was.*

"Now comes the task that each of us must agree to experience. Somewhere locked in the past of each of us—

and it may be recent past—is something that we experienced but only in part were aware of experiencing. In order to learn together, we are going to have to reach down into the depths of ourselves and pull that thing forward. If our attitude is correct, it will come from the Akashic Record; if not, it will be obviously contrived from what our egos want us as well as others to see. It may be that in the viewing of this experience, we will reveal a secret part of ourselves to another but the risk cannot be helped." He paused, searching first Deetra's face and then Curtser's. "Are you willing?" he asked.

Both nodded and said that they were willing.

"Let me first explain that in the physical form we witness life, true life, as a reflection of what actually IS. It is the same as sitting before a sheet of glass and mistaking the reflections seen there for what is actually taking place. Of course, in truth, we are not seeing reality but only the reflection of it and the reflection is both distorted and deceiving. For instance, in the glass, we may see a man walking toward us but in reality he may be walking past us. Let me show you what I mean." Sarpent rose to his feet and rounded the corner of the temple's crystal wall. For a moment it seemed he dropped out of sight. Then an image formed in the smooth glass wall. Both Deetra and Curtser watched it. It was Sarpent's figure moving toward them.

"Where am I?" the Chief Elder called out.

"Directly in front of us," Curtser said quickly.

Deetra knew that it was not so. She could see that they were viewing a reflection but she couldn't see where it was coming from or where it was. It was a peculiar sensation, one that she had certainly experienced before but perhaps had not been aware of experiencing. All life seemed to be that way in a sense.

"Where am I?" the Chief Elder called again. This time his back was turned and his arms were moving forward, away from them.

"You are still directly in front of us," Curtser said.

"And what do you say, Deetra?" Sarpent prodded.

"I'm not sure. My senses say you are directly in front of us," she said, hesitating, confused.

"And what does Soul say?" Sarpent asked.

"That you are coming from behind and simply turned around," she said.

"That is correct," Sarpent said, revealing himself behind them and returning to where they were seated. "Remember, the senses are easily deceived by appearances. You must train yourselves again and again to always tune in on Soul's viewpoint."

"How do we do that?" Curtser asked.

"By becoming aware of Soul's presence," Sarpent said. "It may help you to know that *Soul is the watcher*. It observes, while the senses interact." He paused. It was obvious from his expression that Curtser was still puzzled. "Spend some time in contemplation on the matter," Sarpent said. "Do not rush the understanding but, when you are thinking on what has transpired here, do so by watching the memory of it. Soul will then be viewing the Akashic Record of this event."

"How is it we have lived so long and have not been aware of this reflective vision?" Deetra asked.

"Absurd, isn't it," the Chief Elder said. "Yet circumstances in our daily lives are continually blocking our true vision—until our feet have been firmly set upon the path; when we have yielded to the inner master and asked for divine guidance, then and only then do we begin to free ourselves from the slavery of illusion." He paused, drawing a deep breath. "Notice I said *begin*. As long as we are in the physical form we are subject to the entrapment of illusion. This is because we are subject to delusion, the source of which grows more subtle with each step on the path.

"And now for the experiences of truth," the Chief Elder said. "Who would like to go first?"

Neither volunteered.

Sarpent smiled, looking from face to face. "Then as one who has set the rules, I will go first." He rose to his feet and stood with broad stance, closed his eyes, and began contemplation. He drew his full attention upon the Ancient One, dedicating himself as a channel and asking an image of the Holy One for assistance. For some time he held the image constant and then his memory slipped into recall of a time he stood alone on the platform of Bell Rock. A slow, deathly feeling crept through him, a feeling of fear, and he remembered that it was brought forth because of his concern of who would be the next Hanta. On one hand, he felt that he was the only possible candidate, and on the other, he considered the Lord Casmir from the East. He recognized the cause of the feeling of fear as his own ego.

Sarpent opened his eyes and looked to Deetra and Curtser. Then he sat down next to them. He could tell by their uneasy expressions that they had seen his experience. He had dipped into the Akashic Record and had revealed himself to his students in order to encourage them.

"Who will be next?" the Elder asked.

Curtser glanced at Deetra, who had drifted in thought, and jumped to his feet. "I will be next," he said, bravely.

Sarpent and Deetra sat quietly, tuning in and supporting Curtser in his contemplative silence.

Curtser called upon the presence of the Great One, focusing on the dazzling specks of light radiating from the body of a thin form. It was Ian and yet it was not Ian but the Hanta and he called out to the image with joy at the recognition. The image dissolved but instantly reformed itself. Something was wrong. He could not slip into the Akashic Record as he had been directed by Sarpent. All he could see was the living, radiant ecstasy of the Radiant One.

Sarpent opened his eyes and stared up at the young man. He was not doing as he had been told but still something cautioned him and he dared not interrupt. It was easy to see into Curtser's contemplation. The young man had opened himself as a channel for the others to share his finding in the Akashic Record, yet it was not working. He could not see beyond his recognition of the radiant body of Hanta, only it wasn't Hanta. It was Ian. What was the distortion? What caused it?

Sarpent looked to Deetra. Her focus was interlocked with Curtser's. She was seeing the same thing, or was she? Was Deetra projecting her husband and lover's image to Curtser? Was illusion at work here, rather than truth? He studied both of them with intense objectivity, questioning them as a judge would question and in his fervor the imagery between them stopped.

Curtser opened his eyes and looked down at Sarpent and Deetra.

Deetra as well opened her eyes, glancing first at Curtser and then questioningly at Sarpent. The moment was so intense that it felt as though it was about to erupt. She arose to her feet next to Curtser. "Perhaps it is time for all of us to rest awhile," she said softly.

"Good idea," Curtser said uneasily.

Sarpent did not speak nor look up at them, although he had an overwhelming urge to lash out, to defy the mental atmosphere about them. Instead, he held back and turned the thoughts back upon himself. The consequences were stiffening. He could not move, or speak, or think. He was suddenly locked in a prison of his own emotion.

Deetra and Curtser left Sarpent with the intention of giving him the psychic space to work through the spiritual shock he was experiencing. Both knew that he had not recognized Ian as Hanta, had perhaps refused, and they also knew that the Chief Elder bore the heaviest of burdens in other spiritual areas. He was responsible for all the knowledge that he possessed, and it was his task to carry it in such a way that all who came in contact with him benefitted by it. Next to Hanta, he was one of the greatest channels for the Divine Force. He would recover just as he had recovered from the shock about Lord Casmir, only now his strength seemed somewhat sapped. He required time to himself, to rest.

They started up the long crystal corridor. It was brilliantly lit, yet there was an air of discomfort to it. It was because they were leaving Sarpent behind but, more than that, it was because they were alone. Deetra knew full well that to travel the causal plane on their own could require a complicated length of time. They could easily fall prey to the attractions of the time track and find themselves locked into experiences, perhaps even shocks similiar to Sarpent's in intensity.

She stopped and called out to Curtser who was in the lead. "I cannot go any further," she said. "I'm sorry, but I must stay near Sarpent until he is ready to travel again." A certain tension relaxed as she finished speaking.

Curtser stopped and turned back to her. He did not wish to go on alone. He had been alone, struggling, for what seemed such a long time. Yet he wished to move on, to take the next step in his spiritual unfoldment.

"I'm sure we will meet again," she said, seeing his dilemma. "You needn't worry about that."

Curtser's attention was fixed on his friend. What she said was true. There was a bond between them. They would forever be seeing each other again and again. Yet parting seemed unnecessary this time, whereas the last there seemed to be no choice. He had simply been transported from the Bell Rock platform into the land of the East. Now it was different. He knew that if he was willing, if he could control his impatience, he would have an opportunity for much steadier spiritual unfoldment by observing Deetra's viewpoint. Besides, he was tired of being alone. He wished to share experiences again with someone.

"May I stay with you?" he asked finally.

"Of course."

"Thank you," he said, then motioning with his hand, he signalled her to take the lead.

They turned around in the corridor.

Deetra walked quietly, allowing her instincts to guide her movements. She turned just ahead of the room in which Sarpent sat alone and entered the chamber next to it.

The chamber was larger and it was lighter and the crystal walls appeared less reflective and more transparent. It was filled with the scent of pine and, as they continued in the direction they were going, the scent became stronger.

Curtser caught her by the arm from behind. "Look," he said. "You can see into the crystal."

Deetra was just becoming aware of it when Curtser spoke. The entire wall directly in front of them was the most unusual sight. The wall was not a wall, crystal but not the same as the other walls. It was like an open window into a picture.

The picture was of their village.

It was the Bell Rock gathering place.

Only the picture was not lifeless as pictures were. It was animated, alive with movement. Familiar people were in the scene and they were moving about the area in a deliberate way.

Curtser tugged at Deetra's sleeve. "Are we seeing the same thing?" he asked.

She nodded. "Indeed we are seeing the same thing," she said thoughtfully.

"That man over there," Curtser said, pointing toward the scene, "that is my father. He is delivering grain to the sanctuary behind Bell Rock. Look!"

It was Curtser's father and he seemed to have a feeling that someone was watching him because he turned about quickly before continuing on his way.

"Father! Father!" Curtser called out.

His father seemed not to hear.

"Take notice," Deetra said, "that although we can see what is happening, we cannot hear any sounds."

It was true.

There was absolutely no sound coming from the picture, just activity, and the scent of pine.

Deetra moved closer to the picture. She put her hand upon the surface. It was solid, as though a sheet of glass separated her hand from another world. Slowly, she began to cover the length of the wall with her hand, feeling her way until she came to the Bell Rock platform. It was there that she had become Askan, that the Hanta had welcomed her into the inner circle, and it was there that Curtser had disappeared. She stopped and turned to Curtser, who was next to her.

"What do your instincts tell you?" she asked.

His eyes met her gaze. What did she mean?

"On the journey to Moonwalk, both Rian and I learned how keen your instincts were and we learned to trust them," Deetra said.

"I feel frightened," he said.

Deetra looked deeply into her companion before turning away. She could see a memory forming in him and she could see that he was visibly shaken by it.

She put her hand in front of the platform area. "Intuition tells me that here is the step between worlds," she said thoughtfully. "It is like a doorway, connecting the physical plane with the causal." Deetra took a step forward. "Take my hand," she said.

Curtser took her hand and held it tightly as she moved through the barrier. It was like water, a liquid, vapor-like substance and, when she was completely through it except for her hand that was held tightly in Curtser's, it was obvious that she was straddling two worlds. She was on the platform at Bell Rock although still anchored by Curtser's grip in the causal plane.

She looked about the gathering place. No one seemed to notice her. Then she studied the place on the platform. It was indeed the spot where she had seen Hanta standing when she had become Askan. It was also the same spot where she and Ian had been married. And there was something else she remembered. It was also the spot where the Pink Prince confronted Sarpent, her father, and the Elders just prior to Awakening Day. Somewhere, faintly, she recalled discussion of how the Pink Prince materialized in the physical world. Was this it? According to all she knew it was the place of power within her village. It was the place Hanta was often seen. The positive and the negative forces seemed to materialize here, but not necessarily one or the other. And it didn't seem to require power for the transition either. After all, Rian, Tolar, and Geta had entered. What had they been doing on the platform? Had Rian known of the portal from the scriptures? Then she thought of the Dales and the portal to the East they had shown her and Sarpent. That too was an entranceway between the worlds. Suddenly, her thoughts were all questions, hundreds of them. Quickly, she caught herself, motioning to Curtser to pull her through again.

Deetra was breathing heavily when she popped through the other side.

"Are you all right?" Curtser asked, still holding onto her hand.

"Yes," she said, nodding and releasing herself from Curtser's iron grip. "Just a little out of breath."

"You were frightened," Curtser said.

"No, but uneasy. There was a terrible pressure as you pulled me back from between the worlds."

"Perhaps I should see what it feels like," Curtser said.

"I don't know that I could hold you," Deetra said. "And I'm not at all sure that I could pull you back through."

"But it doesn't seem to me that the holding or pulling is necessary," Curtser said. "If it's a doorway between the worlds, it would seem that one could merely walk through it."

"It seemed that way to me too," Deetra said, "but it didn't feel that way." She hesitated, looking about the room. "I wish Sarpent was available to us. We need someone to guide us through these discoveries, otherwise it'll be forever before our questions are answered."

Curtser looked at her questioningly. He had been alone a long time, had explored many avenues without understanding what he had discovered. It was true that they required assistance but it seemed unlikely that it would come to them.

Suddenly Deetra hurried from the chamber and turned the corner to where Sarpent sat in the next room. The Chief Elder had not moved since they had left him, nor had his expression softened from the hardened, stone-like features they had last seen. The intensity of his suffering was evident and she wished she were able to help him in some way, but she knew that it was doubtful.

She sat next to him, softly chanting the powerful vibration HU. She did this for some minutes, unable to focus her attention anywhere in particular, yet everywhere. A cry for help shrieked out from her innermost being. Then she sat quietly and closed her eyes.

"You could call on your husband Ian," a voice said within her.

"No, I couldn't," she answered back. "I must not draw upon his attention at this time. I must be able to seek help elsewhere."

"And where would that be?" the voice asked.

Deetra did not answer. Instead she remembered Sarpent speaking of the temple of golden wisdom and the great entity in charge there. Perhaps she could call on the master of the temple.

"And who would that be?" the voice asked again.

"I don't know, do you?" she asked.

"It is I, Ramus-i-Rabriz," the voice asked. "Open your eyes and look upon me."

Instantly Deetra opened her eyes and as she did she also jumped to her feet. Standing in front of her was a man slightly smaller than herself, dressed in dark clothes and wearing a broad-brimmed hat. His face was round and his kindly eyes deepset. He was smiling at her.

"I am Ramus-i-Rabriz," the man said again. "I am master of this temple of golden wisdom on the causal plane. What may I do for you?"

Deetra studied the kindly face in front of her. She had never seen anyone quite like this man and yet there was something about the eyes, an expression that reminded her of the Hanta's eyes and also the eyes of another—Malitara Tatz who had visited her prior to her marriage to Ian.

She looked down at the Chief Elder, who had withdrawn into himself, and she thought of Curtser, suddenly aware that he was not in the chamber with them. Then she looked up and gazed into the master's eyes. "Before this journey to the East, I felt myself to be much more knowledgeable than I feel I am now." She paused and in her heart she told the temple master of the Chief Elder and their journey together, their meeting with Curtser, and their discovery of the window into the village.

"Your friend has gone to the other side," Ramus-i-Rabriz said. "He has slipped through the wrinkle in space and returned to the village."

"Will he be able to return?" Deetra asked.

The man with the broad hat did not answer what she already knew. There was always a way back. But for now he was doing what he felt he needed to do.

"You have questions about the doorway," Ramus-i-Rabriz said, turning about and motioning her to follow him. He then led her into the next chamber.

[*108*]

As they approached the image of the village in the crystal wall, she could feel the temple master looking at her.

"I can see by your aura that you have many, many questions" Ramus-i-Rabriz said. "I will try to answer them all in the order in which they protrude from your being." He paused, turning away from her to point to the image in the crystal. "It appears that your village has been singled out as the only spot in which a wrinkle in space or doorway between the worlds exists, but it is not so. Let me first explain what a wrinkle in space is.

"Look here," the master said, indicating a dark spot on the crystal just below the platform where Deetra had discovered the opening. "This opaque spot is an overlapping of space. Always just above an overlapping or wrinkle as I call it, is a tear in the fabric so to speak. The tear is caused by the wrinkle, which has pinched the space so tightly that it opens just above the pinch. This same phenomenon occurs with time as well as space, but not always." He paused, looking deeply into Deetra before continuing. "When the wrinkle occurs it always affects space, but it does not always affect time. Often it does, however. In this case," he said referring to the dark spot on the crystal once again, "only space is affected; thus an opening between the worlds exists without involving differences in time. Actually, there are openings not just here but all over the planet. These key points are easily discernable once you know how to recognize them. For now, you are viewing the wrinkle in space from the other side, which is here in the causal plane. Later you must study the spot from the physical plane."

Deetra was curious about the idea, allowing her attention to momentarily slip, focusing on what she remembered was the same point on the platform. Then she caught herself, returning her attention to Ramus-i-Rabriz who was waiting patiently.

"When time is involved, the imagery will alert you. People's appearances and customs change with the passage of time. They will appear as they had been or as they will be if they are not focused in the present, but you will also know in another way.

"The mind, being an instrument of the lower planes of existence, or beneath Soul, has a mechanism that can tune in very keenly with time passages. It has an automatic clock so to speak and the mind-clock once properly trained is an infallible instrument. It can become so evenly tuned that images of the physical world become completely unnecessary. There becomes a clicking off of the passage of time, which is perfectly lined up with the passage of events. Interesting, isn't it?" Ramus-i-Rabriz said, pausing.

Deetra looked deeply into the crystal image, thinking how unfortunate for Curtser that he had not waited and met the temple master.

"Each in his own time," Ramus-i-Rabriz said. "If one is in a place of learning for which he is not yet ready, he will be drawn to the place of readiness. Your friend was drawn back to his village within the physical realm."

She wanted to ask about the Chief Elder but something within cautioned her. It was not her place to question the traumas of one so spiritually advanced. She knew that in order to know Sarpent's circumstances she would have to live them and that she did not want to do.

Ramus-i-Rabriz was studying her, nodding his head in approval, as if listening to her inner words. "Compassion is the language of the heart in a charitable person," he said. "Sympathy is the language of the fool.

"There is more you need to understand about the wrinkle in time and space," the master said. "Listen carefully.

"As you may have guessed, understanding the wrinkle empowers one with the opportunity to travel anywhere or anytime at will. It provides Soul with the opportunity to experience this anytime, travel anywhere, and thus bear witness to these experiences. And herein lies the great value of knowing these secrets. Soul's mission is to gather experiences that can lead to greater awareness of itself. The more aware Soul becomes of itself, the more God-power can flow through it into the world. In life, it becomes a channel. Life means more than physical body life, although the physical body life is so much more than most realize.

"The physical life entails the allness of all. It is physical or matter; it is astral or emotional; it is causal and it is mental. These forms comprise the psychic body of man. Within this psychic body there is something still greater. It is a speck of the Divine One. This speck is know as SUG-MAD or God. It is a speck of the crystal wall so to speak, since all is interchangeable—the wall of life and the essence of the Great One.

"This speck of the Divine SUGMAD is called Soul, which you have already recognized in yourself as yourself. You have also learned that Soul as the watcher within one's self can also be empowered as the doer. It becomes the doer as it recognizes its capacities via recognition of the Divine. But I can see that some of what I am saying, you are only beginning to grasp. It will come more and more as you ready yourself."

Ramus-i-Rabriz stopped speaking and stood silently facing Deetra. His kindly face and his strong, glowing countenance made her feel very much at peace. Inwardly she thanked him for his presence and for his gentle assistance. She realized there was much in the realm of the Divine One about which she was not yet aware. But she was moving in that direction. It was where her steps upon the path were leading her.

She thought of Ian and she understood why she had been sent on the journey with Sarpent. She knew the reason for herself, and she knew mostly the reason for Sarpent. The Elder was adept at the lower planes of existence. The causal in itself was not a challenge to him, and yet he suffered here akin to any ignorant person. The law was the law. Still her heart went out to him. If there was a way for her to asist him, she would do so.

"There is a way," Ramus-i-Rabriz said.

She looked at him questioningly.

"Love him with full confidence in the Divine way," the master said. "Simply know that he will come out the victor, that he is merely experiencing a test that he will pass, and everytime you feel drawn to help him, imagine him in the arms of the Hanta. He will succeed on the path in this way. It is how you can serve him as a friend and serve the Hanta as a channel for the Divine Force."

"Thank you," she said. The words seemed more from her heart than from her lips.

"And now I have one thing more to show you," Ramus-i-Rabriz said. "If you are prepared."

"I am."

He led her out of the chamber and down the long corridor that she and Curtser had started down before turning back to wait for Sarpent. At the end was a solid wall and to the left of it was an open doorway. The master entered and motioned her to follow.

Inside, neatly stacked on the floor and reaching almost to the ceiling were transparent bags full of a grainy substance. There was nothing else in the room and yet the room had a definite life about it. What was within the bags had an existence, although nothing like she had ever known.

"This is a storehouse," Ramus-i-Rabriz said. "It is a place where unmanifested Souls await experience in the physical world. They will start out as minute particles of space or atoms and then gradually they will evolve through mineral, plant, and animal life until they earn their place as humans. As humans they will continue to evolve, becoming aware of *self* as Soul and Soul as God until they need to exist no more. Through all of this evolvement," the master said, watching the understanding form in his pupil, "all experiences are recorded here on the causal plane. To know anything of the identity of a person or thing, one need only visit the place where the seed bodies are stored. You see, once a Soul is released to begin its experiences, another of its kind remains to record its evolvement. In this way a counterpart of the shattered crystal remains to retain memory. That is how the causal functions within us."

Ramus-i-Rabriz went to the pile and retrieved two bagfulls of the sand-like substance. He handed her one of them. "Perhaps the lesson would be more meaningful if you assisted in the order of distribution," he said. "You may empty this bag somewhere in your village and this one," he paused, handing the other to her, "somewhere around your village. The empty bags must be returned to me. Are you willing to do this?"

"I am," she said, somewhat hesitantly. "But how will I return the bags to you?" She wondered if he would meet her in the village.

"You must return them to me here in the temple," Ramus-i-Rabriz said. "Already you know of two portals or doorways into this land. Surely you can find your way."

The bags were heavy and there was slight movement within. She clutched them tighter. A keen sense of excitement rippled through her. She was to be journeying back and forth into the land of pure memory through the wrinkles in space this unusual *being* had shown her. "I will find my way," she said finally.

"Good. Now suppose you be on your way," he said.

"What about Sarpent?"

"He knows the way when he is ready," Ramus-i-Rabriz said.

Deetra could think of nothing else to say. Her thoughts were still. The only thing left to do was to venture through the doorway to her village in the next chamber. She recalled the unpleasant pull of her previous experience when Curtser was holding her by the hand.

As she began to leave, Ramus-i-Rabriz said: "Release

all thought of the causal as you step into the physical world. That way the transition will be comfortable and simple." He paused, motioning her to leave. "And remember that the reverse is true when you are ready to return," he said.

CHAPTER 8

Deetra stood on the Bell Rock platform, looking out over the gathering place. Everything was still, except for a soft breeze that brushed against her garments, gently tugging at the bags she held in each hand. It was nearly evening and beautifully quiet. Sunset greeted her with a crimson sky. If it hadn't been for the weight of the bags given her by Ramus-i-Rabriz she might have forgotten momentarily that she had only returned to her village to distribute the contents and to study the appearance of the doorway between the worlds.

She needed to know how to return to the causal plane.

Turning about, she looked into space for markings of some kind. There seemed to be nothing, nothing that would distinguish the place until she lowered her eyes to the platform floor.

On the stone was a large circle with a black dot and a long narrow line leading out of it. She remembered it well. The same symbol existed in a cave high on the mountain pass on the way to Moonwalk. In memory she recalled how she had led Rian and Curtser to the cave entrance during a windstorm. Inside, Curtser went ahead to explore and Rian spotted the symbol on the cave wall, telling Deetra of its presence on the Bell Rock platform floor. He told her how as an infant Sarpent would leave him on the platform for safe keeping while he and the other Elders worked in contemplation. He recalled tracing the image of it with his fingers over and over again as he waited. That was all he knew of it then, or all he remembered that he knew. Deetra wondered what he knew of the symbol now. In his work as scribe surely he had discovered something about it. There was no doubt that it had special significance. In the cave it marked the entrance to Moonwalk, which was within the inbetween worlds, and here it did the same. It must have been how Rian had led Tolar and Geta into the causal plane.

Shadows of night began to make the circle indistinguishable. She thought of returning to the sanctuary, to the chambers she shared with Ian. In the morning she would speak with Rian and then she would complete the mission Ramus-i-Rabriz had set before her.

Deetra stretched out on the sleeping mat thinking of Ian. He was not there and yet he was. She could sense that his physical presence had not been there for some time but inwardly her husband was close, had always been close since she had left his side.

She kept the bags Ramus-i-Rabriz had given her next to her and, thinking of her husband, she drifted into sleep. A dream or vision took shape.

It was as though she could see great distances with perfect clarity, yet everything seemed at such close range. It was a peculiar vision on one hand and quite normal on the other. It was as everything looked in daily life. But then she did an unusual thing. Tilting her head upward, she looked down and out across the terrain. It was as though she was viewing life through a magnifying glass and, seeing it in this way, she realized that between the near and the far was a veil and it was the cross-matching of the fabric which, when seen subjectively, made distance seem close. Now, however, looking in this objective way, she saw the veil and how it separated space. It no longer seemed close or flat but, seeing through the veil, it appeared multi-dimensional, and there was more than one veil that registered beyond and increased dimension. She was looking into space this way when she was awakened by a rapping sound.

She opened her eyes and sat up.

The old messenger whom she had grown accustomed to seeing about the sanctuary stood over her, his hands wrapped about a walking stick upon which he was leaning, waiting. It was the stick that had made the rapping sound upon the floor.

"Yes?" she asked, looking up at him, half expecting to see the image of the veil carried forth from her dream.

"The Hanta sends you his greeting," he said, "and a request that you meet with him."

"Where?" she said, hurrying to her feet. Then she remembered the bags Ramus-i-Rabriz had given her and she reached for them. The familiar weight and movement within alerted her to the importance of this day.

"He is waiting for you in the gathering place," the old messenger said. "I will take you there."

The gathering place was as still as it had been the previous evening. No one was about except that Ian was suddenly present and hurrying toward her.

They embraced, remaining close in each other's arms for what seemed a long time and, as they stood lovingly in this way, Deetra recalled her dream of seeing the multi-dimensions of life through the veil and it occurred to her that the veil affected other aspects of life as well. Each dimension had its own feeling and modes of perception and, as she listened to the magnificent range of music from the inner spheres, she realized that each also had its own sound.

"And where would you say we are that we hear this music?" Ian asked softly, lightly kissing her cheek.

"I don't know," she said, aware that he had shared her

realization, "but it is a very lovely place."

"We are in the heart of God," he whispered.

Deetra listened. The music was without image, yet filled with the most beautiful sounds she had ever heard. They were the sounds of love, unfathomable love, perhaps right from the heart of the Divine One. Then suddenly it struck her. Ian had called her to him for a moment of love but also to complete her understanding, which she had acquired in dream form. She was to become aware of the variances and depths of the multi-dimensions as they travelled inward and she could see now how very dense and shallow the physical world was. She understood why Moonwalk or the astral plane had the sounds, shapes, and feelings it had, that the causal was as it was, and the differences beyond. Was there no limit to these dimensions? The answer was a response and it came from deep within herself, echoing forward from a still more inward world. There was no end and no beginning.

There was a tugging within the bags. She became aware of them, realizing that she had unconsciously held them through her embrace with Ian.

He held her at arms length. The weight of the bags drew her arms to her sides.

"I had forgotten momentarily," she said. "I have a mission."

"I know. And now it is time you set out to accomplish it," he said. "You are protected as you are loved, Dearest. Go in the name of the SUGMAD."

She looked long and lovingly at her husband, then simultaneously they both turned and went their opposite ways. Deetra set out for the village where the first bag was to be emptied, according to Ramus-i-Rabriz instructions.

As Deetra hurried down the dirt lane into the center of the village, she thought of her father and how she had not seen him since her wedding day. It had been only since the new moon but it seemed longer. So much had filled her life. Could it be that his life as well had become so full? She came to the fork that would lead to his house and hesitated. There was so very much she would have liked to share with him now but something within held her back. She had to hold her attention on her mission, after which she had to visit Rian before attempting to return to the causal plane. Quickly she set out down the lane again until she came to the center of the village.

The village center was obvious. It was where all the lanes and paths intersected. It was the hub of the wheel, so to speak, and it divided the village into north, south, east, and west. In this way it was nearly impossible for one to lose one's way.

Deetra stood directly in the village center. A few passersby nodded as they moved around her and went on their way. Then she carefully placed one of the bags between her feet so that she had two hands to properly open the other.

She untied the gold band about the top of the bag and opened it. Millions of silver-like sparkling specks seemed to break free, racing out of the opening as if excited to life. She was astounded by their brilliance, like countless miniature stars spiraling out and upward. She stood watching, noticing that as they reached a certain height, they seemed to disperse and break off in little clusters. They spread out everywhere, in each direction of the village, gradually settling on rooftops, in fields, on the cloaks of passersby, although no one seemed to notice. They were, Deetra supposed, beginning the first stage of life. They were matter for the first time and they were very alive in the release of it.

When she could see the star specks no longer, she reached down and lifted the other bag from between her feet. This one was to be distributed outside of the village, according to her instructions. She stood thoughtfully for a moment.

Only one place came to mind.

She would take it into the forest and release it into the Dale's domain.

But should she tell them?

The journey seemed long and tiresome and, within, Deetra argued with herself as to whether or not she would call the Dales to her so that they would be present when she released the unmanifested souls. It was their task to assist lower life forms and to nourish them. Yet no one had suggested that she contact the Dales or anyone else in carrying out her mission. She had been sent back to the physical realm to complete a mission with no specific instructions. She was to use her own judgement as to where the souls were released and to those people she would see along the way. So far she had seen the old messenger, Ian, and a number of unknowing village people. She also recalled how, when she considered visiting her father, something within suggested that she not do so. Of course, that something within was Soul instructing her. It was her higher self. She had learned to listen to it.

Why was it not speaking to her now?

She knew the answer immediately. The trip to the forest was seemingly long because she was functioning from mind, not Soul. Soul was not being permitted to express itself. It was being held back by the automatic responses of her mind. She was rationalizing, reaching for reasons and excuses to do something with a particular flair. She wanted to see the Dales and she wanted to let them know that she had returned, that she had discovered another doorway between the worlds, and to show them the unmanifested souls put in her charge to distribute within the physical world. She wanted them to share in her excitement. After all, it was in the sharing that made an event exciting.

Or was it?

There was a moment in which everything within her became still. Her thoughts ceased as did all impulses and for a moment she stood on the edge of the forest in a state of complete inner silence. She was watching herself. The being within was watching the physical form of herself and it was suddenly in control. Soul had awakened once again to resume its seat of power. Mind, which was operator of thought, was no longer in control. It had returned to its rightful place as a tool, an instrument for Soul.

Deetra did not go into the forest, but stayed on the edge of it. There she opened the remaining bag given her by Ramus-i-Rabriz and set the unmanifested souls free to gain their experience in the physical world.

Rian was not surprised to see Deetra standing in the open doorway to his chamber. He had sensed that she would seek him out and the reason was obvious.

He looked into his friend's beautiful face. Her beauty was not in the shape of her features but in a radiance that seemed to blush out from them. She was a carrier of the Divine Spirit and her countenance was filled with it.

"We have much to tell each other," he said, embracing her in greeting.

"I am curious about how you learned of the opening," she said.

"Well, I didn't really learn of it. I slipped through it, as did the others," he said, moving away, crossing the room to his work table and sitting down. He motioned for her to take the chair opposite him.

Deetra sat down, waiting patiently for her friend to continue.

"We had class in the gathering place," Rian said, "and we went to take a look at the circle on the platform, which I had been telling about in class. He paused, thoughtfully. "Well, Tolar and Geta were the only ones to go with me to see it...." He stopped again.

"And what happened?" Deetra asked.

"Well nothing really happened."

"What do you mean nothing?" Deetra asked.

"It wasn't intentional. I didn't know it would happen," Rian said. "I mean it didn't really happen, and yet it did."

"You are making little sense," Deetra said.

"I know."

"Then please try to explain."

"I showed them the circle and before we knew it, we were with you, Sarpent, and Curtser on the other side. I didn't really know where we were and I certainly didn't know how we got there."

"And the imagination exercise?" she asked.

"Going to the platform to see the circle so that they could better visualize it was part of that exercise," Rian said. "The thing was we didn't try to slip out of our bodies at that moment. We didn't visualize ourselves into the causal plane."

"You must have done something."

Rian looked away uneasily.

Deetra recalled Sarpent's questioning of him, how he believed Rian had followed them, and how Rian then had no explanation for himself. "What do the others feel about the experience?" she asked.

"Tolar recognizes that he has had a spiritual experience of some kind, while Geta feels that her mind has played a trick on her," Rian said.

"And what do you feel, Rian?"

"It was definitely a spiritual experience but, not knowing the nature of it, I have no feelings, except that I know too that it was a physical experience. It happened." Rian paused, reaching for a rolled scroll inside a cubicle above his head. "The only thing I've been able to find in the scriptures about it is here," he said, handing her the scroll.

Deetra unrolled it and read:

[*122*]

*The doorways between the worlds are
everywhere but exist nowhere. They are here in
the presence of the living circle and they are here
in the absence of it. They exist within and they
exist without and they do not exist at all. One
may stumble upon them or one may be shown the
way. The way-shower is the inner master that
each individual has within. Some may hear ITS
voice while some may not. The holy circle is a
clue and a place of power for the initiated Soul.
The Askan reaching this level of beingness is free
to come and go through the doorways at will.
Thus the Askan is the free one of the peoples of
the world.*

That was all.

Deetra allowed the scroll to roll closed in her hand and
raised her eyes to meet Rian's. "I did not expect it to be so
complicated," she said softly.

"There is plenty of time to learn," he said, reassuring
her.

"Is there?"

"Of course."

"I returned to the village on special mission," she said.
"Now that my task is completed, I am to return."

Rian searched her face for an answer and he recognized
her concern. The doorway between the worlds existed on
the platform, but not always. Yet the holy circle marked its
spot. It did indeed seem complicated as she had said.

"Is there not another scroll?" Deetra asked anxiously.

"Another?"

"Yes, one about the holy circle itself."

Rian had not heard of it.

"There has to be mention of the holy circle in the
scriptures," Deetra said again.

Rain appeared thoughtful, his eyes searched distantly
into space. Then he spoke. "Yes," he said slowly, "yes,

[*123*]

there is scripture on it." He rose from his seat and began to look through a stack of open scrolls piled high on a separate work table. "I have seen something," he said, "but I have not studied the parchment as yet."

Deetra waited silently. She did not wish to think and to have her thoughts disturb Rian's concentration.

Finally, he slipped one parchment from the stack and handed it to her. It was titled NOTES TO THE ASKAN TRAVELLER.

> *There are several paths the Awakened Ones can follow. The knowledge of self leads to exploration through the doorways between the worlds. It may be accomplished in one of two ways: via Soul body and/or via physical body. In reference to the latter the former is of course present. The holy circle provides the clue as to which should be used. It provides insight, vision to the other side. It will tell if the physical body can penetrate the opening or if Soul alone must travel. To the traveller BEWARE. If the physical is to be left behind, the mark of the Askan still exists. The mark is a point of fascination for the uninitiated and it draws the hand of the opposing force. Protect your body, bearing in mind that it is the housing for Soul in the physical worlds.*

The scroll ended.

Deetra handed it to Rian, pointing to the place where it mentioned the mark.

He read thoughtfully and then lowered the parchment onto his desk. "And to think I almost forgot this reference," he said. "There are still so many pages of scriptures that I have not read and many that I have not read for a very long time."

"Have you had any further discoveries on the scroll entitled *The Mark*?" Deetra asked.

"No, but I have collected a great many references to

it. The notations made by the unknown hand seem somewhat friendlier now. In a way, I'm grateful to whoever did
it. If they hadn't added to the scroll, I would not have
researched the meaning so carefully."

"I would like to see your research sometime," Deetra
said appreciatively.

"And so you shall," Rian said, smiling.

Deetra rose to leave. "Curtser is here. He has returned
to the village," she said distantly. "I don't know for how
long, but you may see him again."

As Deetra spoke, Rian could see an image of Curtser
slipping through a crystal wall. The wall contained a window into the village. Deetra was seeing in from the holy
circle and seeing from without from the other side. "Where
is that other place?" Rian asked, unsure. "I mean where
were we?"

"The causal plane," Deetra said. "It is the place where
karma is stored and fulfilled and it is the place where memory of past lives are also stored."

"Why are you to return?" he asked boldly.

"Sarpent is still there," Deetra said, uneasily, not wanting to discuss her reasons.

"He asked you to return to the village to do something,"
Rian said, leading her.

"No. Sarpent did not ask me," Deetra said, "and I
cannot tell you more. Please do not ask me. The rest is not
for me to say."

Deetra stood on the platform just above the holy circle.
It was time for her to return to the temple of golden wisdom
on the causal plane. She could feel the presence of Ramus-i-
Rabriz as though waiting, yet something within her resisted.
Reading the scriptures left her with a feeling of helplessness
and she wondered why she had felt it necessary to seek out
Rian. No one had suggested she do so. It had been part of

an analytical process, a feeding of her mental facilities. She had been researching the doorways between the worlds and what she had learned made the matter of coming and going seem more complicated. She had confused herself by placing mind in control. Would she never learn? Mind had tried control over seeing her father and then the Dales. Both times she had caught herself. This time she had not. And it was, it seemed, the most critical time of all.

Looking down, her eyes rested on the diagram within the holy circle—a black dot with a long narrow line leading to the edge of the circle. It pointed to where she had been, only within a different dimension. She lined herself up with the line and then stepped within the circle, facing the edge where the line pointed. Then she imagined the crystal wall, the way it appeared from within, looking out. She began hazily and then the details of it appeared. She could feel the hard crystal floor beneath her feet and see the iridescent glare that the light from the doorway reflected on the crystal walls. Ramus-i-Rabriz stood next to her.

She was there.

"You did well," the temple master said.

Deetra turned to him and quickly looked about the chamber. It had happened. She had returned and, as Rian had said to her about his own journey there, she did not know how she had done it.

"You saw yourself here," Ramus-i-Rabriz said, "but now there is work to do."

Deetra looked into the kindly face. The eyes were all-seeing, all-knowing, yet she felt comfortable with this *Being*. Although he obviously knew everything about her, he did not judge her or intimidate her for being herself. Instinctively she knew that the face was timeless, young and old, soft and hard, gentle and fierce and that, in *Being* all in itself, it knew all—past, present and future.

"Are you prepared to go on?" he asked.

She remembered Sarpent.

[*126*]

"He is occupied," the temple master said. "We will see him again when it is time. For now, we must work alone together."

His words put Deetra at ease. "Then I am ready," she said.

Ramus-i-Rabriz motioned her to sit on an orange cushion in front of the crystal window. She did so and when she looked up she saw why he had directed her attention there.

Tolar was standing on the platform within the holy circle. He began with his hands overhead, feeling downward to his toes within the circle itself. Then he twirled about one way and then another. He knelt within the circle and felt the space all about his body. Clearly, Tolar was searching for the doorway between the worlds.

"He won't find it," the temple master said. "Do you know why?"

"Because he is not ready," Deetra said. "He has not yet awakened to his true self." She hesitated, looking into the kindly face for approval.

"Go on," the temple master said.

There was more to entering the doorway, Deetra knew. She remembered how unsure she had been standing in the holy circle. She had been unsure until she found herself through it.

"Say it aloud," the temple master said.

"I viewed the opening from the other side," Deetra said. "I saw myself here and the rest of me followed."

"That is correct," Ramus-i-Rabriz said. "It is spiritual law that where you see yourself inwardly, the outward must follow. Our friend Tolar is being scientific about it. As long as his mind remains tense in this way, he will not succeed in joining us."

Deetra felt a deep compassion for Tolar, not because he couldn't find the doorway but because she knew how very much he wished spiritual unfoldment. She could hear the inward cry of this man so hungry for God.

"We have the power to draw him through," Ramus-i-Rabriz said. "It is how he chanced this way once before, on Rian's power. A spiritually awakened person's power is great and, the more awakened one is, the greater the power. But riding on another's power is not necessarily the way to unfoldment. If I were to draw him through the doorway, or if you did, we would bear the responsibility of what he would experience as a result of the adventure. Rian now bears the responsibility for Tolar's first journey into the inner planes. That is why it is best for one to be spiritually prepared ahead of time. Of course, it happens on rare occasion that a master will assist a Soul in this way, if the master feels that the Soul can handle the shocks and that the experience will speed up his unfoldment. Still, the Soul would have earned the opportunity." The temple master paused, looking through the window, watching as Tolar persistently searched the platform. "Tell me, Deetra, do you feel that the student has earned the opportunity?"

Deetra examined her compassion for the man. She knew that if it turned to sympathy she would lose control and find herself on the other side with him but, as long as it was compassion she felt, she was all right. Compassion was a detached feeling and not vulnerable to the mind passion of emotion. Then she glimpsed inwardly at the nature of the student.

Tolar had sought her help in connecting with the Elders and with Hanta. She had turned him down, telling him that he would find his way through his resources. And she knew that he had not yet found his way and that he was now at the point of desperation. Yet would a visit to the causal plane assist him in any way? He had already been there under Rian's power. What he needed was a linkup with the Hanta and that he would draw to himself by merely being ready for the linkup. He was in desperation now, nearly utter despair. If only he would quit pushing at the door, so to speak. If only he would allow the door to swing open. Perhaps his despair would bring him to that point when he would give up after his long search.

It was as if Tolar had heard the words of Deetra's heart. He suddenly stood up and, as though in utter despair, he turned about and walked off the platform, heading back for the village.

He had given up.

What had she done?

"You assisted your student," Ramus-i-Rabriz said. "You made it possible for him to see himself from your viewpoint. Although he does not know why, he knows he must surrender, give up after such a long vigil of trying to make something happen."

Deetra looked after him, noting that his head hung low as he walked and his shoulders slumped. Then she turned her attention again to the temple master.

"No, do not look at me," Ramus-i-Rabriz said. "Look again to your charge. The student is about to receive a gift from God."

Deetra looked. Although Tolar's heart was heavy with defeat, there was a certain poise that he seemed to regain. His frame straightened as he walked quietly. Then he stopped. The old messenger approached, standing in front of him and in his hand was a crystal. It was the same as had been given to Deetra long ago when she first started her adventures toward Awakening Day. The old messenger motioned that Tolar take the crystal and then said, "It is Hanta's gift to you. What you do with it will be your gift to Hanta." Then the old messenger turned away and left Tolar standing there. Deetra could see the excitement glow within him. Always he had the Hanta in his heart, but now the Hanta had him in his heart.

She turned to Ramus-i-Rabriz. He was smiling at her and she was smiling back, deep rich smiles that swelled from the heart and glowed from their faces. The joy was shared as their eyes met.

"And now for some very fine points of spiritual law," the temple master said. "You had a right to assist the student Tolar because inwardly you had a pact with him, but what about offering assistance to one with whom you have no pact?" The smile had faded and his expression was serious again.

"I don't know," she answered.

"Of course you do. Think about it! You must learn to think more, consciously think before speaking. It is the activity that ignites Soul's attention," he said firmly.

She sat up straight as if trying to better understand. It was true she had answered that she didn't know without first thinking.

"Think about it. When you are ready with the answer we will continue," he said. Then he turned his back to her to leave her alone.

Deetra's mind grew suddenly alert. It raced about trying to grasp her sudden circumstances. She had been told to think but now mind was not thinking but reacting to the temple master's chastisement. Momentarily she was out of control. She focused her attention at the point of her spiritual eye, just above her eyebrows and to the center of the forehead, and kept it there. It was the seat of Soul. Then gradually the silence came and she took command. She began to think of her right to help Tolar and what it would be like to offer assistance to one with whom she had no right. Clearly she saw that to offer help to one who did not want it would mean that she was invading their personage, their psychic space. That person would rightfully exchange the difficulty for the deed and she would be stuck with their difficulty. The magnitude of her thoughts struck her.

"It is called the law of non-interference," Ramus-i-Rabriz said. He turned toward her as he spoke and rose to his feet, motioning her to follow. "Now I will show you an illustration of this law," he said. "Prepare yourself."

Deetra did not know what to expect, following Ramus-i-Rabriz out of the crystal chamber and down the long corridor. They stopped in front of a narrow doorway and entered.

The walls appeared to be crystal as were the other chamber walls but instead of a window to the village she saw that the crystal was a looking glass, reflecting her image in a full 360 degree circle. Oddly enough, the temple master, although he was standing next to her, did not reflect in the glass.

"This is where the Akashic Records are kept," he said, watching as she discovered some of the nature of the chamber for herself. "The records are not volumes of parchment as you would expect. Nothing is ever written down and therefore no scribe is necessary to maintain them."

Deetra thought of Rian and how he would appreciate this manner of record-keeping.

The temple master smiled at her thought, motioning her to look about the chamber.

There was Rian, working at his writing table in the sanctuary office. He was studying the scrolls Deetra had read when she was last there.

Deetra looked to the temple master for some explanation of Rian's presence.

"It was the thought you just had about Rian," Ramus-i-Rabriz said. "Your thought triggered the memory bonds and brought the image of Rian at work just after you left him."

She looked at the master in amazement.

"It is all here," he said. "Everything that ever has been IS. Tell me, Deetra, how do you feel about Rian's concern for the notations on the MARK scroll?"

She hesitated, unsure. Although she had felt his concern interesting, she did not feel the same concern as he did. The notations in brackets seemed to be honest statements and to her it mattered little who made them.

"All right," Ramus-i-Rabriz said, "but you have never

imposed your feeling on him?"

"No."

"But let's suppose you did. Suppose at the height of Rian's interest you went to him and gave him advice on the matter." The temple master paused, waiting for the image to formulate in her mind. When it did, it also appeared on the looking glass walls that encircled them.

Deetra was amazed. It was as though she had entered Rian's chamber, finding him hard at work. He was researching any and all references to the MARK that he could find in the scriptures. It was exactly as she had remembered, just following her marriage to Ian.

She interrupted Rian to tell him that his concern was useless, and that there was much more to be learned via a positive approach to the scroll, than with a negative one. It seemed a small matter at the time and Rian did not appear overly ruffled by her comments. But as the scene disolved, another scene took form. It was Deetra learning from the old messenger that she was to accompany Sarpent on a special journey.

"Just how do you think your assignment came about?" the temple master asked.

"I don't understand," she said, distantly, studying the image of herself in the reflection.

"Then let me show you a scene recorded long ago as another example," the temple master said. He waved his arms and pointed to the looking glass about them.

An overweight little girl sat on a log, watching as the other children played about her. After awhile another little girl came up and sat down next to her. It was Deetra. Little Deetra began telling the fat little girl how nice it would be if she would lose her ugly weight, that she could then join in the games of the others. As it was, being fat made it seem that the girl lacked balance and could not keep up with the others.

In the weeks that passed, to everyone's surprise, the

fat girl began to lose weight and Deetra began to gain it. Something else happened to Deetra. She showed poor balance in the game and seemed to lack the stamina to keep up with the others.

Deetra was astounded by the memory. It was true and she remembered with terror the feeling of being unsure of herself in the company of her friends.

"Do you remember what finally saved you?" the temple master asked.

The gradual image of her father presented itself. He realized her difficulty and drew the problem out of her, helping her to eliminate it.

Then why didn't the difficulty stick to him?

Deetra knew the answer almost immediately after she thought it. He was her father and it was his responsibility to assist and protect her, and their union was by an unspoken but mutual agreement.

The looking glass images faded and Ramus-i-Rabriz turned to Deetra. He smiled. "I can see by your silence that you understand," he said gently.

She nodded, too astounded to speak.

"Of course, your interference with Rian's lessons made it possible for you to advance your own," he said.

She looked into the kindly face.

It was true.

She would not have been here, learning under the guidance of the temple master if she had not interfered. She was paying off a karmic debt by learning lessons she was required to learn. The law of non-interference was very strict.

She thought of Rian. She could see that it was his task in life to be scribe because of the education he would derive from the task. Her lessons were to come mainly from other levels of existence, or so it seemed. It was easier to see another's circumstances than it was to see her own.

"When you understand the causal plane, you will have living knowledge of the seed body of your life, as well as a general awareness of this knowledge in all lives," Ramus-i-Rabriz said. "You will have instant awareness of the effect of all causes and you will have the ability to pick and choose so that you will live as cause and determine your effects on the environment.

"You will also have the power to transmute the forces—both positive and negative into the middle or neutral force. Here all life rests in a state of balance and it will be within your power and right to set it that way. It is how great souls work as channels for the Divine Force." The temple master paused and turned about on his heels. "Let us see the balance you now possess," he said.

Turning about in the direction in which the master had turned Deetra was again caught by surprise. She had believed that the chamber was devoid of anything except them and the looking glass, but now directly in front of her was a deep abyss with flames leaping from the center of it. A log, not more than eight inches round, was stretched across it. The distance it spanned was more than three times her height.

"You are to walk the log and cross to the other side," Ramus-i-Rabriz said. "There you will find a doorway through which you are to enter. There a greater test than this one awaits you. At the far end of the second chamber is another door. I will meet you on the other side."

Deetra stared at the abyss unable to move. Her body felt frozen and her breathing uneasy. She did not dare look at the temple master directly but through a keener vision she saw him noting her composure and she was very much aware of when he turned and left her alone.

She did not know how long she stood on the edge of the abyss, watching the flames leap upward, wrapping their long red-orange tongues about the log she was to cross. She felt for a time as though her body was paralyzed, as if she was struggling to fulfill the task Ramus-i-Rabriz had set before her, but regretfully could not. She wanted to, but could not move.

If only the temple master had remained to encourage her, but she was alone, or so it seemed, and she had never been so completely aware of her aloneness as now. Then she saw something she had not seen. The flames were not merely tongues leaping around and across the log she was to cross but they were actual tongues of fire and they were eating the log. It was smoldering, weakening with every moment she waited. If she allowed her terror to continue to hold her, she would forfeit the opportunity and fail. She had come so far, too far to fail now. She was married to the man who served as Hanta. How could she permit herself to fail? Most of all, she would fail herself as a spiritual being.

Instantly, her fear vanished, transmuted into courage and determination and she stepped upon the log. She moved slowly, unsteady at first. The flames threatened, leaping upward about her feet and legs. She hesitated, realizing that the fury of the fire could not harm her. It projected no heat to her and therefore no pain. It was true the log had been burning, but it seemed to cease to burn the moment she stepped upon it. The abyss was not an abyss but an illusion of some kind and she continued moving across the log with sudden ease, like a child playing a game.

When she reached the other side she found herself standing on a narrow ledge. She paused again, looking about, noticing that the fire was raging again, tearing at the log with sudden fury. Within minutes it had eaten through it. The log cracked and fell into the abyss. There was no return. What had seemed an illusion seemed real enough now. Then she saw that near her was the door to the next chamber and it was ajar, as though welcoming her through it.

Deetra moved through the open door with slow, even movements, the door inching its way closed, pushing up against her to close at her back. The darkness appeared instantly, total darkness, and she dared not move. Her hands behind her back, she tried pulling at the door to let in light from the other chamber but it had fastened itself tightly and she could not budge it.

She did not know which way to go.

Was the doorway she was to exit through straight across the chamber or on another wall?

She decided it would be straight across as the other one had been.

She took one step and stopped.

There was a moaning sound. It was soft at first but, as she stood trying to identify it, it grew in magnitude. It sounded like a roaring wind. It suddenly tugged at her hair, her clothes, barely making it possible for her to stand erect. She stood as still as possible, dropping finally to her knees to steady herself in the dark wind.

Someone laughed.

It was a hideous laugh, and it grew louder, darker, more hideous. It was black laughter.

Deep chills rippled through Deetra as she waited. The sound was familiar although she had never heard it. There was memory to the laughter. The darkness of it betrayed an evil smile and she remembered standing with Curtser long ago on Moonwalk, being a part of his experiment with the Pink Prince's jewel. The Prince had come to her in a vision from the pink jewel and in it he threatened that someday he would dominate and destroy her. It was because she had discovered his secret. He who was called the Prince of Love was really the Prince of Darkness. He used people's emotions to trap them. Rian had once been dominated by him and Curtser and many from the village. She had been among the few who would not succumb, one of the few who caused his downfall.

The laughter rose in pitch and penetrated her. It was as though she was hearing the cells of her body cry out and they rattled like a serpent's deadly tail.

"You cannot evade me!" a mighty voice echoed throughout the thick dark chamber. "I have sworn to destroy you and destroy you I shall." The voice roared in laughter again. "You are my prisoner now."

Deetra was aware that the more attention she paid the Prince the more he could dominate her. She tried to think of something else, remembering how, when Curtser was trapped on Moonwalk, she sang to him until his attention broke free from his mock prison. She began to sing to herself now, not the village songs she had used then, but the song of all life she had learned from Ian during their wedding procession. HUuuuuu ... HUuuuuuu ... HUuuuuuuu ... Over and over again she sang the sound. The Prince of Darkness faded and to her astonishment a burst of light filled the room.

She had to tightly close her eyes at first, then gradually she opened them and rose to her feet.

It was beautiful.

Autumn-gold trees shimmered in a soft breeze, caught by rays of sunlight. Nearby was a pool of pale blue water and children were playing at the edge of it. She could hear their laughter and shrieks of joy, and her eyes trailed the thick green grass-carpet that gently rolled in every direction. Occasionally a leaf fell and, when it did, it sounded like a faint tinkle in the ethers, a sound of something yielding to the change of season. If it had been a day in the village with Ian, it would have been a perfect day, but it wasn't. It wasn't a day in the village.

Deetra looked about skeptically. She was still within the second chamber of tests. She had transmuted the Pink Prince into the scene now before her, but she was not sure what the true nature of what the transmutation was.

What was she seeing?

Had the HU eliminated the remainder of the test?

Was Ramus-i-Rabriz here, waiting for her?

At that moment there was a child's scream. She looked

in the direction of the pool. There was no one there. The children had seemingly gone and yet the scream came from that direction. The scream came again and then once again. Deetra tensed and started for the pool, then abruptly caught herself.

The screaming continued. Was she to be the witness of a child's drowning? Would she do nothing? There was a part of her nature that was tearing at her, pulling her in two directions. If she were in the village she would not hesitate to answer a cry for help. In this illusionary world she did not know what to do. She must not be drawn by negative forces and yet she could not stand to ignore a child's distress call. She must help if she could help, but then she reminded herself that this was not an episode in life.

She began to sing HU again. This time it was filled with the pain she was feeling from the distressed child. Over and over and over again she sang HUuuuuu ... HUuuuuuu ... HUuuuuuuu. Then suddenly the child stopped screaming.

Deetra looked in the direction of the pool. It was difficult to make out what she was seeing at first—children but not children. They had appeared that way from the back, but now they had turned around and were approaching her. Their faces were not faces but outlines of total blackness and, as they moved through the golden forest, the leaves turned away from them, withered, and fell to the ground. They too had turned black. Soon the whole forest was withered and dark.

Deetra caught her breath.

Next to her were the creatures with the black faces. There were no features to them of any kind, just blackness, like deep pits. They were not children at all, or any form resembling human, except that they had bodies and outlines of heads. For some reason, she thought of the Dales.

Of course, they were not the Dales. The Dales were gentle invisible creatures, but for some reason they came strongly to mind. She recalled last seeing them at the portal to the East. They had told her to remember their secret and shared a special way of calling their power into being. She remembered it and she called it now.

"Daaa-lles ... Daa-lless," she called strongly.

The creatures stopped in their approach and reached out to her. They seemed to be made of wax, to melt one into the other right before her eyes, ending in a pool at her feet. The Dales had said that to use their name in that way called upon the neutral energy and now Deetra had an idea of their power. The pool before her was not actually wax, nor was it water, but lightening quick to move at any impulse or change in vibration. She supposed that it took on the Dales' vibration since their's was the power that transmuted it.

The light in the chamber was dimming and the air took on a musty scent. Deetra felt an urge to move on toward the doorway on the far side of the chamber. She could see it now, a slick, black door still some distance from her. She headed directly for it.

"Deetra! Deetra!"

Deetra turned about in surprise. Starn, her father, stood on the edge of the now black forest. He appeared to be hurrying and short of breath.

"My daughter, what you see is not an illusion. You are seeing the circumstances of the village. Curtser has returned and with him came the power he both carries and opposes. Ian is in grave danger and is being held captive."

Deetra looked deeply at her father, caught by his final words. "Who holds Ian?" she asked cautiously.

"Lord Casmir claims the Ancient One passed him the Rod of Power and that he now bears the title of Hanta," Starn said.

Deetra stared at her father in disbelief. They both knew Lord Casmir was the Pink Prince. How could the negative force overpower the positive. After all, it was Ian who was the Hanta.

"All I can tell you is all I know, my daughter," Starn said. He lowered his eyes sadly, as if hurt by his daughter's distrust. "It is not my will that the circumstances are as they are."

"How did you find me here?" Deetra asked.

"You are my daughter."

What Starn implied was true. There was a bond between them and in like manner she could track him down as well if she felt it necessary. She recalled a time when he was ill and the negative force came to claim him in a dream. Deetra had witnessed the dream and had interceded, protecting her father via their bond of love. Still, she had to be sure. She was in the chamber of tests. Ramus-i-Rabriz had warned her that the second chamber's tests far exceeded the difficulty of the first. What she had experienced so far was beyond the incredible. Her emotional control was being constantly tested. It was doubtful that her husband was in any sort of danger.

She looked deeply into the man who said he was her father. "In the name of the Divine SUGMAD, I ask you to identify yourself," she said firmly.

Instantly, there was a change in the appearance of the man. It was not Starn but Lord Casmir and he stood firmly, undaunted in her presence. "It does not matter who stands before you," he said. "The circumstances are the same. Your husband Ian has been weakened by illness and I have taken over his domain."

Deetra lowered her eyes, not humbly but rather because she did not care to place her attention on the Lord Casmir's toothy smile. She would not accept his play with words. As Hanta, Ian would survive no matter the circumstances. If he did not there would be nothing that she could do. He was the representative of the SUGMAD, the Godman.

"But you do not understand," Lord Casmir said, knowing her thought. "As distributor of the positive force, the

Hanta cannot use the power for himself."

Deetra could feel that the Lord Casmir was still smiling, waiting for response. She would not give it. She was in the chamber of tests. She could not allow this abominable creature to stir her emotions, which would make her fail. She remembered that at the critical moment in each test, she had been saved by chanting the HU. She began to sing it now, placing her full attention upon it and moving as quickly as she could toward the doorway to the next chamber.

She reached it.

The door was smooth as she had seen it in the distance, but what she hadn't seen was that it had no handle. Her heart cried out for an answer and she turned about quickly as if to see if the answer was behind her. It was not Lord Casmir that she saw, but the Radiant One, the Hanta.

The Great One stood before her in full brilliant light and out of it came the most beautiful music. She recognized both the light and the sound. It was the force of life, the SUGMAD in manifestation. It was Ian, but not Ian the man. It was Ian the Hanta.

Her mind groped somewhere inside of her, drawing forth the memory of where she was. She was in the chamber of tests, trying to find the way to open the door that would reunite her with Ramus-i-Rabriz, and suddenly the Hanta was here before her.

She had to be sure.

Perhaps it was a trick of the negative force.

The Hanta seemed to be waiting patiently.

Deetra closed her eyes so that she could not see the Radiant form and softly sang the ancient name for God. "HUuuuuuu ... HUuuuuuu ... HUuuuuuu," she sang, and inwardly she called on the Mighty One to dispel the illusions about her. Gradually, she felt at peace and opened her eyes.

Still in front of her was the magnificent, radiant form of Hanta.

It was not an illusion.

It was the Mighty One.

"What may I do to succeed in this test?" Deetra asked humbly.

"Go back to the first chamber of tests," the Hanta said.

Deetra's heart froze. Never had she been so overcome. She could not go back to the first chamber. She had come so far, had endured so much, that she feared her courage was wearing thin. To go back there could mean that countless pitfalls awaited her—the darkness, the horrors—and she remembered too that the crossing log in the first chamber had been burned through. How would she reach the other side?

When the surge of fear had subsided, the image of Hanta had disappeared. She looked about the chamber. She noticed that the smooth door without a handle did indeed have a handle now. She could reach for it, pull the door open as she had originally been instructed. It was there she was to meet Ramus-i-Rabriz.

But NO.

Hanta had said for her to turn back.

Was she to obey Ramus-i-Rabriz or was she to obey Hanta?

It was Hanta!

She hesitated, pulled in two directions, searching deeply within herself for an answer. She wished so very much to grab the door handle and end this maze of tests and it was this feeling that reassurred her to follow Hanta's request. Ending it all now would be a relief, which would appease the emotions. She was an Askan. She was a free spirit, accountable only to the SUGMAD, to the Hanta.

It was her answer.

She turned around and, following the Hanta's instructions, she set out to return to the chamber where the tests had begun.

To her surprise, there was no going back. She was there in the first chamber without retracing her steps and without incident. Ramus-i-Rabriz stood in front of her. His expression sober and serene.

"And now you have earned the right to know the secret of your initiation," the temple master said, "and with it comes certain responsibility. Are you sure you are ready?"

She drew herself fully erect with a long, deep breath. "Yes," she said, "I am ready."

"Good." The temple master smiled and motioned her attention to the looking glass walls. They were totally blank, and it appeared that they were transparent in part and solid in another part.

She did not know how long she stood there staring at nothing. She did not see herself reflected there, or any other image.

"What have you learned of this chamber?" the temple master asked.

She wanted to answer that she did not know or that she was not sure, but instead she instructed herself to reflect and to think on the matter before speaking.

She remembered the Akashic Records and how the looking glass was the reflected images of those records, how they had showed her an interaction with Rian and how her intrusion on his interpretation of a scroll prompted her to venture into unknown regions with Sarpent. She regretted interfering with Rian's thoughts on the subject but at the same time she was glad that she had liberated this opportunity for herself. She doubted that everyone on the path to God had the same experiences. She also knew that it was not necessary for everyone to have the same experiences. It was her attitudes that made it necessary for her to experience certain things.

She paused in her thoughts and looked into the temple master's serious face.

"Continue," he said quietly. "The realization you are

[*143*]

reaching has not yet unfolded completely."

Deetra focused her attention on the center of her forehead, on her spiritual eye, and drew her focus deeply within. She sensed a new reality close about her. It was a reality of varying degrees and the feeling of it seemed the most prominant. The feeling suggested herself as a seed body, that everything she was, everything she thought, everything she did, was the effect of her *being*. There was no way to intellectualize on the subject, nor was there any way to really describe it in thought. It was beyond thought and words, but not beyond perception. It could be felt as a whole, a reality, and it could stimulate awarenesses in countless other areas. It promoted freedom by consciousness and that consciousness enveloped the world about her.

"You have the secret," Ramus-i-Rabriz said, "but still you must learn the magnitude of your awareness."

She looked into the kindly face, now serious. What could she do to reach the magnitude. Life would have to show her, magnify her experiences through dramatization, episode after episode. It was these episodes that were filed in the Akashic Records. They were the cold, hard facts of her life and how they interacted with others. She did, however, have an advantage. She was aware of how it worked, and her awareness carried with it the Divine power to transmute the negative energy into positive and it also empowered her to function as a balancer within the environment at large.

"Yes!" Ramus-i-Rabriz said, listening to her thought. "And now that you know, you bear the mark of the enlightened one. The mark is indelible. It is the power, the wisdom, and the love bestowed upon those who have proven their readiness. The mark is visible to all who approach and yet its form is formless. The presence of one who wears the mark is graceful with power, wisdom and love, which is charity, and all who approach recognize this. Recognition of a mark-wearer does not mean that he who recognizes will accept, without question or rebellion. The rebellion may be fierce, such as the attraction of an opposite force. They who wear the mark are the chosen ones and are protected by the positive forces, as long as opposing thought does not invade. It is the responsibility of the mark-wearer to exercise control at all times. The mark once placed can never be removed. It is the heaven of he who serves the Divine forces and the hell of he who finds he cannot." Ramus-i-Rabriz stopped speaking and looked deeply into Deetra.

Deep within the master's gaze, Deetra saw a tiny image of herself and in the image was a memory. The memory was the scroll Rian had given her. It was a copy of the original entitled the *MARK*. According to her memory, Ramus-i-Rabriz had just recited it.

Then it struck her.

It was no coincidence.

Rian had given her the scroll of the *MARK* because of some inner prompting of which he was not aware.

He had given her her lesson on the causal plane, and perhaps his own.

Then she remembered.

What of the inscription in brackets? The scroll had been written in one hand and the words in brackets by another.

Ramus-i-Rabriz laughed. He threw out his arms playfully and slapped his thighs with his hands. "You still don't know," he said. "I can see that you still don't know."

Deetra studied the temple master. He was obviously enjoying a laugh on her, but why?

Then it dawned on her. Ramus-i-Rabriz must have made the notations in the brackets.

The temple master looked at her seriously for a moment, allowing her realization to come through, then he burst out laughing again.

Why was he laughing?

"I am the author of the MARK," he said flatly, "and the notations are mine as well."

"But how?" she asked. "They appear to be written by two different hands."

"And indeed they are," Ramus-i-Rabriz said, smiling as he held both of his hands out in front of him. He looked first to one, opening and closing his hand as he did so, and then to the other, repeating the gesture. "It's a technique I use to lure the curious. It is how I lure those ready to learn into learning," he said. Then he smiled broadly. "It is the poet in me."

Deetra looked upon the temple master in a way she had never done. She saw him suddenly as one with human nature and one with a keen sense of humor. She was grateful for the glimpse into this great being and out of her gratefulness she felt love. "Thank you," she said, sincerely.

Ramus-i-Rabriz nodded. "You may now pass on from this land, with full knowledge of how the lower worlds operate," he said. "You will return many times as a wayshower to those who require assistance in getting here and for other purposes now unknown. I bid you well, Deetra." He raised his hand in farewell. "Go with the SUGMAD," he said.

Ramus-i-Rabriz vanished.

CHAPTER 9

Deetra stood alone in the looking glass chamber, waiting, as if Ramus-i-Rabriz might reappear. She had no immediate direction. She could, of course, at any time return to the village but something within her hesitated. She did not know why she was still in the temple but she was. Perhaps she was still here to absorb something more, to experiment perhaps with the looking glass, or to return to the chamber that fostered the doorways between the worlds to discover something more, or perhaps she was to gather up more unmanifested souls and distribute them in the physical world.

All of these things seemed like possibilities but none spurred her to action. She stood there alone as if waiting for directions.

None came.

She listened with an inward ear. The soft tinkling of bells was superimposed over a thin, piercing high-pitched sound. She had come to recognize the latter well. It was the sound of SUGMAD reaching Soul. It was her sound, individualized, and it came constantly to her inward senses whenever she listened in that certain way. The other sound—the bells—were reflective of where she was. The bell was the sound of the causal, the seed body sound, perpetually called to life as the universal mind triggered thought sequences throughout the physical and astral planes.

There was no end to it, she knew. The little bells would ring perpetually, as long as life continued its unfoldment. But there were other sounds from other planes as well.

She listened to her sound, the high-pitched one of her individual identity, and she thought of Ian. Although she was alone, she knew of his presence. She knew of the presence of Ian the man and husband, and she knew of the presence of Ian the Hanta. They were inseparable and yet they were not the same. She thought too of Rian, of her father Starn, of Curtser, Tolar, and finally Sarpent. Her thoughts had not wanted to touch on Sarpent, to interfere in any way in the settlement Soul was making within him. She did not know why Sarpent could not accept Ian as Hanta and she did not care to know. Sarpent was a spiritual giant among ordinary men. He had been stern and steady in his unfoldment toward God Realization and had, she supposed, earned the great rite.

Or had he?

Suddenly Deetra caught herself. She was beginning to look into the Soul of Sarpent, to see his torment and why it existed. Ian was Hanta and Hanta was the Godman. He was the SUGMAD's representative. Perhaps Sarpent was suffering to reach that realization only now.

She stopped.

Mind seemed to be leading her and she did not wish to follow mind. She had no business delving into the Chief Elder's affairs. His state of consciousness had nothing to do with her.

Or did it?

They had travelled to this place together. What was their connection? She seemed to feel an answer rise from deep within herself and she pushed it back, quickly rejecting it before it could reach her consciousness. She did not wish to know the answer now and yet she was drawn to it. Turning about, she left the looking glass chamber and set out down the long corridor to rejoin Sarpent.

[*148*]

She stood in the reflective chamber where they had last been together, where Sarpent had instructed her and Curtser in the art of seeing through fine illusion. It was where they had experimented with memory experiences, where Curtser envisioned a meeting with Ian the Hanta and Sarpent denounced it as a lie. She had expected to find Sarpent still there. It was where she had left him to his inward suffering. But he had gone.

But where?

She turned about to see if some illusion had frozen itself in the crystal wall but there seemed to be nothing except waves of light, multi-colored and multi-dimensional. It was difficult to see into the wall of illusions because the perspective held no single viewpoint.

"Sarpent!" she called, examining the walls. "Sarpent, can you hear me?"

There was a long silence in which she heard nothing but her own sound of Soul and the tinkle of bells. Then, faintly, a voice answered her.

"I am here, little sister," the voice said.

It was Sarpent's voice.

"But where?" she called back. "Where are you?"

At first there was no answer. She thought back to Sarpent's earlier instruction in the chamber. He had said to her and Curtser that *somewhere locked in the past of each of us is something that we experienced but only in part were aware of experiencing*. He then declared that each would have to *reach down into the depths* of themselves and *pull that thing forward,* that pulling forward would be the facts stored in the Akashic Records.

"I'm caught on the other side of illusion," Sarpent said finally.

Deetra noticed that, as the Elder spoke, a wave of light passed through the crystal wall. It quickly disappeared as he finished speaking. "It is not possible, Lord Sarpent," she said, watching for the impulse in the crystal to form again.

"But it is," he said. "I know the illusion but I cannot seem to break free of it."

It was then that Deetra saw where the wave of light began. It was almost directly in front of her and she was certain it marked the spot of Sarpent's entrapment. "How did you get in there?" she asked.

There was another long pause in which the waves of light moved about agitatedly. "I was testing myself," Sarpent said.

"In what way?"

"Spiritual powers are not to be discussed," the Chief Elder said.

"Then how can I help you?" she asked.

"You cannot," he said.

Deetra was not to be defeated. "Use your contemplative powers," she called out firmly. Suddenly it was as though she was the Elder, as though they had switched roles.

Sarpent did not respond to her command.

"Use your contemplative powers," she called again. "Reach back into your memory bank and draw forward the experience holding you captive."

The silence was longer than before and Deetra sensed that the Chief Elder was retreating, going further into himself and the illusion that held him there. "Your refusal is keeping me from my husband," she said loudly. "Ian awaits me as the Hanta awaits you!"

She fell silent, watching for the waves of agitation in the crystal wall but there were none. The light seemed absolutely still. Quickly she focused her attention inward, on the spiritual eye in the center of her forehead, and placed an image of Sarpent there. Gradually the animation began. She saw Sarpent moving boldly through the dimensions of crystal, pushing his way deeper and deeper into the folds of illusion. Then she had an idea, if she dared.

She saw herself in the illusion, standing in front of

[*150*]

Sarpent and blocking his passage. The Elder roared toward her, his spiritual powers raging devastation in its path. She alone could not withstand it and in this knowledge she quickly called upon the Great One to assist her.

The Hanta in all his radiant glory appeared to block the rage from Deetra's path. It did not bounce off the Great One but it seemed to be absorbed and transmuted, flowing through him and returning to Sarpent as love.

Sarpent fell to his knees, weeping.

The Radiant One disappeared.

As though in a dream, Deetra moved toward the weeping Sarpent. She knew the gravity of his pain. The crystal's colors seemed to dart about, reflecting the emotion he was feeling. "Let it flow free," she said, gently touching him on the shoulder. In her spiritual eye she saw the nature of the bittersweet pain Sarpent was enduring. It appeared first as the wave of love that the Hanta returned to him in exchange for his rage and then, as if pieces of shattered glass were torn away, she saw the reason for his great shock, the reason he could not accept Ian as Hanta.

The Akashic Record produced a scene of Sarpent and Ian and in it the Chief Elder was criticizing Ian for not bowing down in the Hanta's presence. He called him a pompous ass and suggested that his lack of humility was due to his lack of spiritual unfoldment and awareness.

The scene faded.

Sarpent buried his face in his hands, weeping.

Deetra lowered her eyes. She did not feel criticism for the Chief Elder and she knew that Ian did not either. What the Elder was feeling was the return of the flow he had projected. In calling Ian the pompous ass, he was recognizing the pompous nature within himself. It was his lack of humility and his lack of awareness and spiritual unfoldment. And now, he had to accept this fact or accept self-destruction. His ego held him prisoner and Deetra looked with compassion on what she saw. Ego was the last of the passions of mind to let go. She had heard frightening tales of its tenacity and how in its resistance it twisted a person's perception, thus warping his viewpoint toward all life. She had never met one so afflicted until now and she did not know how to help.

"Go back to the village," Sarpent said, wailing through cupped hands. "I don't need you here."

Deetra lowered her eyes again, cautioning herself not to fall into sympathy with him. If she did, she might find herself in the same predicament.

"Get out of here," Sarpent snapped. "Leave me at once."

A deep sadness enveloped Deetra and she felt she could not leave. She stood quietly, her head lowered, calling out to the Hanta in her heart. As she envisioned the Great One's radiant form she understood the real meaning of love and compassion. It enveloped her now and she wished she could pass the awareness of it on to Sarpent. But she couldn't. No one could free Sarpent but Sarpent and the Elder was aware of that fact. Deetra could not remain in the causal worlds trying to help him. To do so would mean that she was accepting his karma and the burden was not for her to share. She would only hurt herself and in the hurting still not help him.

"May the blessings be!" she said, raising her eyes to look upon the desperate man. Then she turned about and made her way out of the crystal wall.

Sad and thoughtful, Deetra found her way back to the doorway between the worlds. She paused before it, looking into the village gathering place. A rush of people seemed engaged in some activity. They were moving here and there about the place, their attention drawn occasionally by a fierce gust of wind. She didn't see what they were doing but then her thoughts were not with them, but with Ramus-i-

Rabriz and his explanation to her about a wrinkle in the fabric of space and time. What she had experienced upon using the doorway was coming and going through a wrinkle in space. The temple master had said that the imagery was different when time was involved. People's appearances and customs change with the passage of time. But what if the time period was basically the same. If only a year had passed there would be little difference in appearances. It seemed that one wouldn't know if a wrinkle in time was being encountered or not, unless one was to witness familiar scenes and people from another time in the past.

Deetra studied the images of the village people in front of her through the crystal window. Nothing appeared out of the ordinary, except that she didn't recognize any of those present, nor did she understand the activity in which they were engaged. Slowly it struck her that she should have recognized the people. There was no one in her small village she did not know or who did not know her.

She looked again.

She knew no one.

The gathering place was the same. The speaker's platform seemed no different, and she could almost make out the holy circle etched upon the floor but not quite. The angle was somewhat illusive, but it appeared to be as she remembered it. Her eyes scanned the environment. Nothing had changed in the mountainous horizon, which surrounded the valley. The evergreen forest where the Dales resided still rose at the foot of the mountains. It was true something was different, but what?

Then she saw it.

A large black drum was being dragged into the marketplace. Following it was a man she supposed to be of great importance. He stood tall and erect, his long dark robes flowing in the wind. Behind him was an older man, his face buried in his hands, weeping.

The older man was Sarpent.

Her attention snapped back to the man in the long black robes. He turned as if to acknowledge her unspoken question and nodded. It was Lord Casmir.

Quickly Deetra turned about, withdrawing her attention from the gathering place. She didn't know why she had seen what she had seen nor did she wish to know, yet she knew she had to know.

She turned back to the crystal window and, as she did, she sang the powerful vibration HU. The scene that she had witnessed a few moments before vanished before her eyes. She recalled how the sound had dispelled the illusions in the chamber of tests, how each time an image disappeared when she sang it meant that the encounter was an illusion. And now it seemed the tests continued at the opening of the doorway between the worlds. This time the illusion had involved Sarpent and as she thought of the Chief Elder she knew that although it had been an illusion, it wasn't. He was being held prisoner by a memory, but his captivity affected much more than himself. It affected the entire village. If she were to return there now, she too would be affected by it. The karma of one so influential affected the karma of the whole. She had to help the Elder for himself and for everyone else. She would interfere as a channel for the Divine Force for the good of the whole.

She had an idea.

Perhaps there was a way to erase the memory that held him prisoner. It would be a form of transmutation. It was the powerful secret of the causal plane.

Deetra hurried back into the chamber where Sarpent was hidden within the dimensions of crystal wall. She stood confidently. "I have found the way," she said, calling to him.

"Little sister, why do you torment me?" he called back.

"To free you."

"But you cannot. I have told you to leave me and return to the village."

"And I cannot return," she said.

There was a long deathly silence. The wave of light within the crystal was decidedly agitated.

"Just now when I went to the doorway I was confronted by an illusionary scene. In it were unknown people with Lord Casmir as their supreme one and you, grovelling behind him," Deetra said, quickly spitting out the words as though she expected to be interrupted. "You could not expect me to enter such a scene."

Sarpent did not answer.

"If I had tried to use the doorway between the worlds," she said, "I would have entered your illusion. Can you not see that your state of mind has affected more than yourself."

"That is impossible," he roared back.

"Is it? You are the Hanta's most valuable agent. Your spiritual powers are incomprehensible. Your thoughts and actions have a great affect upon others as well as the environment."

"It cannot be!" Sarpent screamed.

"But it is!"

"The Hanta has it in His power to remove my influence," Sarpent said, "and he will."

"No," Deetra said softly. "I don't believe He will." She hesitated. "To remove your influence would be to destroy you and your awareness of SUGMAD."

"Then so be it," Sarpent shouted.

"No!"

Deetra drew in a long, deep breath. She knew she was running the risk of offending herself by attempting to assist Sarpent, but there seemed no other way. She could not return to the village in the state she last saw it under Lord Casmir's rule and she did not think that the Hanta would intercede. To do so could interfere with lessons others required for their spiritual unfoldment and it would damn Sarpent, thwarting the opportunity for this great personage to awaken to some grand degree. She knew she had to help

Sarpent and she knew that, in helping him, she ran a risk but also that she could benefit too.

"Have you forgotten the nature of the causal plane?" Deetra called to Sarpent.

The Chief Elder did not answer.

"You do not have to accept the memory that plagues you," she said again. "You can recognize the root of your actions and through recognition, rip it out." She paused, waiting to see if the Chief Elder would respond, but he didn't. "Only you, Sarpent, can uproot your own actions and words."

"What would you have me do?" he asked coolly.

"Be honest with yourself," she said.

"In what way?"

She knew that he was skirting the answer, not wanting to face what needed to be done. "You cannot accept Ian as Hanta because you feel he is beneath you," she said.

"That is not true," he said, snapping back angrily.

"Why then?" she prodded.

Sarpent did not answer.

"You called him pompous and belittled him for his lack of humility," she said, reminding him.

Sarpent wailed as though in great agony.

"Well, didn't you?"

"Yes. Yes, but you don't understand," he said.

"Understand what?"

The sobs of the Chief Elder sounded like wretching, as though a part of him was being pulled apart.

"Understand what?" she asked again.

"I am the pompous one," he shouted back. "I am he with no humility. The villagers stand in awe of me, not the Hanta. They fear me and the power I possess, not the Hanta. Never have they felt this way toward Ian. I was the one with prestige." His breath caught, sobbing, and he stopped talking.

"Why then were you against Ian?" Deetra asked, trying

to push him still closer to the truth.

The sobbing stopped and there was a long silence in which it was evident that Sarpent was collecting himself. "The Ancient One always favored Ian and I wished that favor for myself," he said humbly. "I understood why the Hanta favored him. He had completely given of himself, which was something I could not yet accomplish. There were certain things in my nature that held me back." He paused, looking inwardly before he continued. "Pride held me back. I looked for my faults in Ian and accused him of them. It is said that ego is the last of the mind passions to dissolve and it appears that I have proven it."

With the last breath of confession, Deetra relaxed. Sarpent was no longer hidden in the crystal wall of the illusion of dimensions. They stood together in the chamber, gazing at each other with love and gratitude. Sarpent had thrown off the burden that so sorely affected him, Deetra, and so many others, and she could see from the look of relief on his face that the release had empowered him with the God Force.

Slowly Sarpent's face grew solemn and he looked deeply into Deetra's eyes. He seemed to be seeing something there of which he hadn't before been aware. "You are a great little lady," he said softly. "Did you imagine that you would come to this greatness as a child?"

In the imagery beneath his words, Deetra knew that the Chief Elder was not flattering her person, but suddenly struck by the fact that she had married the man who served as Hanta. She nodded. "I believe I did, but not in any specific way" she said thoughtfully. "I just knew something special was going to come into my life, but I didn't know what."

Sarpent's expression changed to one of compassion. "Ahead of you are great challenges, great enough to match the greatness of the role you have accepted."

"I know," she said, nodding.

[*157*]

"Traps are set everywhere," the Elder said, "and, as you can see from what I nearly succumbed to, they are subtle, lurking in the shadows of a small place where unawareness still exists, in a place where mind has refused to surrender its passion." Sarpent grew silent and pensive, looking deeply at Deetra but also within himself.

A chill rippled through Deetra as she felt the Chief Elder's gaze in this way. She knew what he said was true.

Suddenly Sarpent became aware of the impact of his feeling upon her. She was shaking in the reverberation of his spoken and unspoken words. He smiled at her, wrapping an arm about her shoulders to comfort her. "Let us not worry about tomorrow, little sister," he said. "We have conquered today and so let us be victorious." He turned to face her again. "Besides, we Askans have help," he said lightly. "There are masters about us everywhere we go and they are always willing to show us the way."

Deetra relaxed. What Sarpent had said was not only comforting but true. The great master of the causal plane, Ramus-i-Rabriz, had shown her much. He had guided her with explanations of how the causal plane functioned, explaining the Akashic Records, the time tract, the doorways between the worlds, and how unmanifested souls became manifest to relive the cycles of worldly experience. And she knew, too, that the Hanta was always at her side, gently guiding through her intuitive ear. And she remembered the strange adept Militara Tatz who appeared to her following her decision to marry Ian and how he had promised to guide her at a time when he would be needed. That time was still to come. The traps ahead were great, she knew, but there were many to help her succeed. She knew that she now had a friend in Sarpent as well. Perhaps someday he would prod her from danger as she had done for him. The bond between them was now evident.

A tugging at her gown turned her around.

Sarpent had drawn her attention to the doorway between the worlds.

Standing on the platform within the holy circle was the Radiant One. He stood with outstretched arms, beckoning their return. The globe of light seemed to reach through the doorway, embracing both the Chief Elder and Deetra. They were enfolded by it, drawn within, where there was only intense light and indescribably beautiful music.

They were home again.

THE END, BOOK TWO

"Life is a dream but the dream has become so commonplace we cannot see it."

ORDER FORM

Please send me
the following book(s)
by Heather Hughes-Calero

No. of copies	Title	Price	Amt.
_____	THE GOLDEN DREAM (hardcover)	$16.95	_____
	THE SEDONA TRILOGY: (trade paper)	7.95	_____
_____	Book 1 **Through the Crystal**		_____
	Book 2 **Doorways Between the Worlds**	7.95	_____
	Book 3 **Land of Nome**	7.95	_____
	TOTAL		$ _____
	Shipping: (1 book $1.00, 50¢ per book additional)		_____
	California residents add 6% sales tax		_____
	TOTAL ENCLOSED (Check or money order) USA FUNDS ONLY		$ _____

please print

NAME: _____

ADDRESS: _____

CITY, STATE, ZIP: _____

_____

COASTLINE PUBLISHING COMPANY
Post Office Box 223062
Carmel, California 93922
(408) 625-9388

Also available at your book store.

place
stamp
here

COASTLINE PUBLISHING COMPANY
Mailing List
P.O. Box 223062
Carmel, California 93922

place
stamp
here

COASTLINE PUBLISHING COMPANY
Mailing List
P.O. Box 223062
Carmel, California 93922

If you wish to receive a copy of the latest Coastline Publishing catalog/
brochure and to be placed on our mailing list please send us this card.

Please Print

Book in which this card was found _____

Name: _____

Address: _____

City & State _____

Zip: _____ Country: _____

If you wish to receive a copy of the latest Coastline Publishing catalog/
brochure and to be placed on our mailing list please send us this card.

Please Print

Book in which this card was found _____

Name: _____

Address: _____

City & State _____

Zip: _____ Country: _____